D0958658

ALSO BY JOSEPH F. GIRZONE

Joshua
IN THE
HOLY LAND

JOSEPH F. GIRZONE

SCRIBNER PAPERBACK FICTION
Published by Simon & Schuster

SCRIBNER PAPERBACK FICTION
Simon & Schuster Inc.
Rockefeller Center
1230 Avenue of the Americas
New York, NY 10020

First Scribner Paperback Fiction Edition 1995

SCRIBNER PAPERBACK FICTION and design are trademarks of Macmillan Library Reference USA, Inc., used under license by Simon & Schuster, the publisher of this work.

Manufactured in the United States of America

10   9   8

Library of Congress Cataloging-in-Publication Data
Girzone, Joseph F.
    Joshua in the Holy Land / Joseph F. Girzone.—
1st Collier Books ed.
        p.   cm.
    I. Title.
    [PS3557.I77J65   1993]
    813'.54—dc20   93-6525   CIP
ISBN 0-684-81344-0

This book is dedicated to those rare individuals who have been able to rise above self-interest and personal ambition to bring the presence of God and His peace into our troubled world.

ACKNOWLEDGMENTS

I would like to express my sincere gratitude to Peter Ginsburg, my agent and good friend, for his continual support and valuable assistance. I would like also to express my appreciation to the staff at Macmillan: Barry Lippman, the president; Bill Rosen, the publisher who personally did a most sensitive job in editing this difficult manuscript; Bonnie Ammer, Judy Litchfield, Richard Dojni, Norm Adell, Pat Eisemann, Patrick Sadowski, Susan Richman, Marie Marino, and Melissa Thau for their professional expertise and friendship, which I shall always treasure. The artists who designed the jacket deserve special praise for their thought-provoking portrayal of the essence of the story. The copy editors and proofreaders have my heartfelt thanks for their painstaking work. And not to be forgotten are my dear friend Elie Zambaka and his family, whose deep commitment to their faith has been a constant inspiration, and also my dear friend Monsignor Tom Hartmann, for his insights and constant support.

1

A BLAZING SUN beat upon the desert sands, painting strange images across an overheated horizon. A lonely figure walked with determined step along a trackless path toward his destination. His loose brown pullover shirt, his tan pants, his sandals seemed out of place in the desert. Only his desert headgear seemed to fit the scene. He was humming a light tune as he walked briskly along, looking here and there as if for something to distract him from the monotony of the barren wasteland.

Off to the right a young lamb staggered along the top of a dune, confused and obviously lost. The man walked toward the frightened animal, bent down, cuddled its head between his hands, and rubbed its ears gently. The animal didn't resist, merely looked up at him as if pleading. Picking up the lamb, he placed it on his shoulders, and continued on his way.

Hills of sand stretched endlessly on every side. How could anyone find his way in such a place, with no reference points? But the wanderer pushed on, knowing precisely where his steps were leading as if he had lived here all his life. Over one more sand dune, then another, and finally in the distance, an oasis: tall palm trees shooting majestically from the sand, tents spread like giant mushrooms around a pool of cool water that glistened like an emerald in the setting sun.

An old man sat pensively on an Oriental rug before a fire, with legs crossed, smoking a water pipe. His face was thin and taut, his fingers gnarled and tough like leather. The stranger approached him, and bowing, greeted him in Arabic, "Salaam aleichem, my friend. My name is Joshua. Wandering through the desert I found this lamb walking aimlessly. I thought it might belong to your family, so I am leaving it with you."

With that, Joshua took the lamb from his shoulders and placed it on the ground. The lamb spotted a little girl about nine years old and immediately ran over to her. The girl noticed it and screamed in delight.

The old man turned toward Joshua, eyed him critically, looking deeply into his eyes, and introduced himself. "My name is Ibrahim Saud. These are my family," he said as he proudly motioned with a sweep of his arm toward the hundred or so people milling around the camp. "I am grateful to you for bringing back my granddaughter's lamb. It is her pet and has been lost since early morning. She has been crying all day. I would be honored if you would stay and eat with us. It is getting dark, and the desert is treacherous. Sleep here for the night. It will be safer."

Children were walking timidly toward Joshua from different directions. When he noticed them, he turned and smiled. Gradually they walked over and surrounded him and the old man.

Speaking in Arabic, Joshua asked their names. The girl who owned the lamb told Joshua her name was Miriam.

"That is a beautiful name," Joshua told her. "It is my mother's name."

"Is your mother beautiful?" the girl asked as she kept stroking the lamb in her arms.

"Yes, she is very beautiful," Joshua answered.

"Where did you find my lamb?" she asked. She eyed

Joshua from head to foot, noticing how different he looked.

"Not too far away, just over that hill and the next one beyond," Joshua responded.

"Was he looking for me?" she continued.

"He was looking everywhere but could not find you," Joshua reassured the girl, to her delight, then continued, "Couldn't you tell how glad he was to see you?"

"Yes, he means more to me than anything in this world," she told him. "He was my birthday present. My grandfather gave him to me."

"Isqar, your look tells me you have a thousand questions to ask me," Joshua said to a boy who kept staring at him.

"Yes," the boy replied, surprised that the stranger knew his name. "Where were you coming from, and where are you going? People don't just wander around the desert. The nearest bedouin family is miles away from here, and you aren't one of them."

"I am just passing on, stopping here and there wherever I am welcome," Joshua told the boy.

"Where are you going?" the boy went on.

"Visiting places I remember from long ago," he replied.

"From long ago?" Isqar said, surprised. "You're only a young man. How could you have been here long ago?"

Joshua laughed. "I may be older than I look."

As Joshua continued talking to the children, a wiry young man whose face was bronzed and wrinkled from constant exposure to the sun approached the old man.

"Father, that man is not one of us," he blurted out angrily. "He's a Jew. How can you show kindness to an enemy? How can you share with him our family hospitality?"

"My son," the old man said calmly, "I don't know he's our enemy, and he doesn't look very Jewish to me, though I suppose you are right. His accent is Jewish. Do you have any reasons that would convince me he is our enemy? He did return the child's lamb. He did not even ask for a favor in return. When you grow as old as I am, my son, you will see things the young cannot see. This man is not an evil man, nor is he an ordinary traveler. Allah walks in his shadow. As soon as I looked into his eyes, I saw the presence of God."

"In a Jew, Father?" the young man protested.

"Allah does not see Jew or Arab," his father answered. "We are all formed by the hand of God, fashioned in God's heart. Whoever opens his heart to His goodness, Allah blesses them with His presence. And this man is close to God. There is no evil in him. It is when we hate we drive God from our heart, and become like broken tools. Then we begin to do the work of Satan. Now, go, Khalil, my son, and leave me in peace. Your anger troubles me deeply."

Others in the family, just as curious as the children, began to encircle Joshua, asking him all kinds of questions. They were all wondering what a Jew was doing wandering the desert full of Arab bedouins.

Joshua took their questions good-naturedly, laughing at their last concern. "I walk through the world as a pilgrim. I have no hatred in my heart. I see a child of God in everyone I meet. My innocence threatens no one. Where I see hurt, I heal, if the heart is open to God's healing. Where there is no room for God, I walk on."

"You're a strange man, pilgrim," one man said. "Where are you going?"

"Passing through," Joshua replied, "wandering through places I remember from long ago, remembering the events that happened here."

"You are heading in the direction of Jerusalem. To visit Jews?" the man continued.

"To visit whomever I meet along the way. To bring God's message of peace," Joshua answered patiently.

"Do you think people will listen to your message of peace, pilgrim?"

"Yes, people want peace. Only sick people thrive on hate. Someday, however, when fathers learn to love their children more than their hatreds, then peace will come."

Khalil overheard Joshua's comment but said nothing, merely smirked cynically.

Miriam's lamb left her side and walked over to Joshua and started nibbling at his toes, which were exposed between the sandal straps. Joshua bent down and picked up the lamb. Everyone was surprised that the lamb took so easily to a stranger.

"See," Joshua said, "the lamb makes no distinction. Neither does God." The animal relaxed in Joshua's arms.

The old man had been listening to everything that transpired, and smiled as the lamb fell asleep in Joshua's arms. He called out to his wife, who came immediately.

"My husband, you called?" she asked.

"This stranger has found our child's lamb," the old man said to his wife. "Prepare a place for him at supper. He will be our guest tonight. Prepare a bed for him as well. It is not right that we send him out into the darkness of the desert."

The woman shot a furtive glance at Joshua, who was watching her. She left and disappeared into one of the tents, with some of the women following her. They were all curious about this stranger. She could tell them nothing more than her husband told her, and that he would be a guest for the night. The women, too, were surprised that the sheik would welcome a Jew.

The supper turned into a celebration. After the sun set, a cool breeze swept through the camp. Lamps hung on poles lighted up the oasis, creating a festive air. Simple instruments, most handmade, were used for the music. One woman played panpipes that held the whole family spellbound. Men danced spontaneously with one another. Some of the more friendly ones even grabbed Joshua to dance with them, which he did and enjoyed immensely. The fragrance of meat heavily laced with garlic cooking on a huge spit filled the atmosphere. Wine flowed freely.

When the party ended, everyone was ready for sleep. In no time, a vast chorus of snores broke the silence of the cool desert air. Everyone slept soundly.

In the middle of the night, the quiet was shattered by a child's piercing scream. Lanterns and flashlights were turned on in every tent. A little girl was crying uncontrollably, pointing to two tiny punctures on her arm. With his flashlight one of the men found the snake slithering out from under the tent. Running outside, he clubbed the viper with a shepherd's crook. It was a deadly snake whose bite was almost always fatal, especially for a child. Bedouins feared these deadly creatures more than their worst enemy. They struck without warning in the dark of night when no one could see them. People went to sleep at night in fear, wondering and praying about these snakes that wandered unseen and unheard in the darkness.

There were no doctors in the camp, and no medicines that would help. Without hospital care the girl would surely die. But the nearest hospital was a two-hour journey by camel. One old four-wheel truck wouldn't be much faster, even if they could find their way in the dark.

Awakened by the commotion, Joshua walked over to the tent where the girl was still screaming. Her arm was turning redder each minute and was extremely painful. Women wailed, and children cried in fright, afraid to walk on the ground in the dark.

As Joshua entered the tent, the girl's father was asking everyone if they had any experience with such a thing, or any medicine that might be a cure for the deadly bite. No one could help. The old man was standing next to Joshua, who seemed so calm. "Joshua, on your travels, have you learned of anything that might save our little girl?" Ibrahim asked his guest.

"Once, a very long time ago, I came across a family who carried medicine with them as they crossed the desert," Joshua said. "Has no one here any medicine?"

"No one," the old man said.

"Then trust God to heal her," Joshua said quietly.

A woman nearby laughed cynically.

"Young man, I have faith. I trust Allah, but would He heal a snakebite?" Ibrahim said to Joshua, not questioning but wondering if God would concern Himself with a matter so trivial to Him.

"Nothing in a child's life is trivial to God. He loves you and cares tenderly for you. A child's life is not a little matter. It is precious to God. If you trust Him, He will help your child," Joshua said reassuringly.

"I do trust in Allah," Ibrahim said, "and I also know that you are a holy man. I could tell the moment I met you. Can you help? Is there something you can do for our child?"

"Do you believe strongly in God?" Joshua asked.

"With all my heart," the old man answered, to which the whole family boldly assented. "We believe in Allah. Do you think He will help our child?"

"Just trust Him." Joshua walked over to the girl, who was sitting on her mother's lap, and touched her badly swollen arm, saying simply, "Little one, be well."

Immediately, the swelling went down, and the pain ceased. The two bite marks disappeared, and the girl relaxed and slowly stopped crying. Her mother hugged her frantically, almost smothering the little girl between her breasts.

The whole camp was overcome with awe. Ibrahim's initial respect for Joshua was more than vindicated. He thanked Joshua profusely and pledged his family's eternal gratitude. Joshua tried to downplay this display of his powers, attributing it to God's care and the family's faith. After a few minutes the camp was quiet again, as everyone retreated to their tents. Khalil was the only one not impressed. He was sulking in the corner of the tent, more angry now than ever that a Jew could be an instrument of

God, and that his family now owed a debt to a Jew. The old man noticed the look in his son's eyes and grew sad.

The rest of the night was long, as everyone found it difficult not to imagine creeping things crawling through their tents. Joshua fell asleep immediately, to the amazement of everyone in his tent.

As soon as the sun rose, the camp came back to life and in no time was buzzing like a hive of agitated bees. People looked at Joshua with almost a reverence, which only his lighthearted humor was able to dispel. The little girl had no trace of the snakebite and was busy playing with her friends. After their breakfast of various cheeses and fruits and coarse bread and strong, sweet coffee, Joshua prepared to take leave of his new family. Though they had known him but a few hours, they had already learned to love him as one of their own.

The old man kissed Joshua on both cheeks and hugged him like an old friend. "Joshua, you are welcome in my family at any time. You have saved the life of our little child. My whole family is in your eternal debt. Should you ever need us, we will give our lives for you." The sheik removed a gold coin from deep inside his robes. "Only twelve such coins have ever been minted. Twelve coins for twelve saintly men. Wherever you go among Arab people they will respect this medal," Ibrahim told Joshua. Joshua accepted the gift, and read the words inscribed on the face: "Forever our friend. May Allah protect him," and on the reverse, "Sheik Ibrahim Saud." The old man placed it around Joshua's neck and kissed him.

"May God bless you, my friend, and your whole family for your kindness to me," Joshua said gratefully. "I shall never forget you. And I know that one day our paths will cross again. Till then, may God walk in your midst."

Miriam ran over to Joshua and threw her arms around him. Joshua bent down and hugged her.

"Thank you, Joshua, for finding my lamb, and bringing him back to me. I will never forget you."

Joshua walked out of the camp into the desert. A teenage boy ran out to him. "Joshua, Joshua, I want you to have this," the boy shouted, holding out a container of water.

"This is my favorite canteen. I've had it since I was a little boy. I want you to have it. It's full of cold water. The desert is hot and you will need it."

Touched by the boy's thoughtfulness, Joshua thanked him and, caressing his face, blessed him. "God will richly reward you, Isaac, for your kindness."

Joshua walked off. The boy stood there watching him as he disappeared over the hill, surprised that he remembered his name. Everyone knew he was walking toward Jerusalem, and wondered.

CHAPTER 2

JOSHUA PUSHED onward in spite of the heat and hot, coarse sand that washed through his bare toes with each step. This was the way it used to be, he remembered; territory so familiar from long ago, isolated villages little changed through the centuries, though the original ones were now buried deep beneath piles of sand and rubble. The people were still the same, hardened by the harshness of life, but hospitable and kind, mostly Arabs now, but no different from the Jews of old. People are not much different from one another. Events and circumstances condition their behavior, and most humans respond predictably when subjected to the same treatment.

Joshua's path out of the desert took him into the Judean hills. Passing ancient Beersheba, he wandered through the rolling hills of Shephilah and stood above the famous site where Goliath and the Philistines encountered Saul's army of Israelites. Standing on the hill of Socoh, Joshua surveyed the bowl-shaped Valley of Ela and could easily envision David walking boldly across the valley to meet the Philistine giant. He could see David carefully aim his sling-shot at the laughing Goliath and watch it strike him square-ly on the forehead, thus winning the day for the Israelites. Leaving this, Joshua approached the site of ancient Emmaus, now called El Qubeibeh by the local inhabitants, and a Sabbath day's journey from Jerusalem along the western slope of the Judean hills.

Walking into the village he saw a crowd of villagers gathered around a cow or a steer that had just been slaughtered or had been hit by a careless driver passing through town. The townsfolk were busy dividing up the carcass and carrying off portions in wheelbarrows. Flies were everywhere and almost completely covered every chunk of meat.

As Joshua passed by, most were too busy to notice him, but one man standing off to the side looked over as he passed and in shock commented, "Hey, there's a Jew walking down the street."

Everyone stopped, all noise ceased. Every head turned toward Joshua. The same reaction as that of the bedouins the night before: stunned disbelief that a Jew would dare walk in their midst. A few laughed, some made insulting remarks. Taking their cues from the grown-ups, the children picked up stones to throw at the intruder.

Joshua made no move to defend himself, but instead called each of the children by name, "Ismael, Iqbal, I met your friends Ahmed and Isaac in the desert last night. They told me all about you and said what good friends you have been."

The boys were shocked and ashamed and dropped their stones, and just stood there as Joshua approached.

"Why would Ahmed and Isaac talk to you, a Jew?" the boys questioned.

"I stopped in their camp last night, and their grandfather extended hospitality," Joshua answered calmly.

Iqbal noticed the canteen Joshua was carrying, and excitedly pointed it out to Ismael. "Look, he's carrying Isaac's canteen."

"How did you get that water container?" Ismael asked angrily, suspecting foul play.

"Isaac gave it to me as I was leaving the camp this morning," he replied.

By that time, some of the men had walked over to Joshua and the boys. "What are you doing here, Jew?" one of them asked bluntly.

"I am just a pilgrim passing through, visiting places I remember from long ago," Joshua answered patiently. "I bring no harm to anyone, just peace and Allah's blessing to those oppressed."

"You're a strange man, pilgrim!" a rather thoughtful man interjected, disarming his companions and shifting the conversation to a more friendly tone.

"What sites are you looking for?" the same man continued.

"There was a house here I stopped at many years ago, long before your time," Joshua replied.

"Which house?" another asked.

"A house by the side of the old highway that passed through here on the way to the sea," Joshua answered.

"There is no highway passing through here to the sea," another middle-aged man said sarcastically.

"There was at one time," Joshua said, looking straight into the man's eyes.

"And you visited someone here then, I suppose," a fat man said, laughing.

"Yes, they were relatives and good friends. The highway went right past the side of their house," Joshua replied matter-of-factly.

By then the men were beginning to think this stranger had something missing upstairs, and they all began to laugh at him.

"Don't be too quick to laugh," said the thoughtful one. "Up near the church are the remains of an old Roman highway that used to go from Jerusalem to Jaffa, on the seacoast. And in the back of the church are preserved the ruins of an old house that once stood there. The priest told me the whole story one day."

The man was one of those strange paradoxes in the Holy Land, a Christian Arab, and remembered the Bible stories his priest had told the people so many times.

"How would you know about that place?" the man said to Joshua. "Are you Christian?"

"Yes," Joshua replied simply.

"But you're a Jew!" the man answered, confused.

"Yes, and you are an Arab. Which kind of Christian is more surprising, a Jew or an Arab?"

The man laughed.

"I will show you the place, if you like," the man offered.

"I would like that," Joshua answered gratefully.

The two men walked off, with a couple of the others following close behind. Most of the others went back to their dead animal and continued dividing it among themselves.

As they approached the church, Joshua was struck by the beautiful rose garden surrounding the courtyard in front of the church. An Arab man was conscientiously tending the bushes with great pride. A priest in Franciscan robes had just emerged from the church and was walking down the stairs to the courtyard when Joshua and his companions approached.

"Salaam aleichem, Daoud," the priest said in friendly fashion.

"Salaam, Father," the man replied, and Joshua followed suit.

"What can I do for you?" the priest asked.

"This man just came into town and wanted to see a house he used to visit, a house that sat next to the highway," Daoud told the priest.

The priest was caught off guard and seemed mystified.

"My friend, Daoud, there are no houses like that around here," the priest said.

"What about the one in the church, Father?" Daoud asked.

"What about it? This man certainly couldn't have visited friends there. That house hasn't been lived in for centuries, almost since Jesus' day."

"But Father, how did he know it was here?" Daoud pushed further.

"What was the house like, young man, the one you visited?" the priest said to Joshua.

"It was a small house with tile floors," answered Joshua, going on to describe the tiles in exact detail.

"Have you ever been in the church?" the priest asked.

"No, I haven't, Father," Joshua replied.

"Amazing! You have described the house so perfectly, and yet you have never been in the church. Come, I will show you," the priest said as he guided the group into the back of the church.

There in the back left-hand corner was the house Joshua described. Joshua turned and looked at the remains of the house, deeply absorbed in his thoughts. A red cross on the wall placed there by the earliest Christians marked the site as one authentically associated with Jesus' life. The men stood there a few minutes watching Joshua as his eyes passed along the tile floor and scanned the stones in the wall.

"Who was it you were visiting here, young man?" the priest asked Joshua.

"A couple I met along the way. They were relatives," Joshua answered.

"What were their names?" the priest persisted.

"Clopas and Simeon," Joshua said.

"Where did you get Simeon from? He is not mentioned in the Gospel story. Have you ever read the Gospels, Joshua?" the priest continued.

"No," Joshua replied.

"How, then, do you know the story?" the priest asked, baffled.

"It is not a story. It is a memory I treasure," Joshua

answered calmly, as the three men exited the church.

The priest did not know what to make of this odd pilgrim and the things he said, so he concerned himself no further.

Outside the church were the ruins of the old Roman highway, constructed of black tufa stones neatly laid next to one another. Grass had grown between the stones and all around them. Only sections of the road were exposed, but enough was visible to delineate what were clearly the remains of a very ancient highway. Joshua looked at the stones and followed the road with his eyes toward Jerusalem, remembering clearly that late-afternoon meeting with the two disciples who were on their way to Emmaus, and his playful encounter with them as he met them at the crossroad and hid his identity from them.

The whole story of Joshua visiting this house, and his knowledge of the existence of the highway, was not only baffling, but totally incomprehensible to the priest, who could only surmise that this stranger must have at some time or other visited the church as a young boy, and confused the details of his experience in his mind over the years. Daoud, however, wondered about Joshua and how he knew so much about the house when he had not seen it in God knows how long.

The priest shook hands with the two men and wandered off toward the garden where he began conversing with the gardener. Joshua and the Arab walked to the gate of the compound. Daoud gave Joshua a little piece of paper with his name and address on it and said he hoped their paths would cross again. After talking a few minutes, the men parted, going their separate ways.

Joshua continued on his journey toward Jerusalem, detouring through Bethany first before approaching the city.

Bethany was still only a small village on the eastern slope of the Mount of Olives, not more than a mile and a half from Jerusalem. Joshua walked around the site of Mary and Martha's house and the tomb where Lazarus was buried.

The original buildings were no longer to be seen, but the tomb was still there, the oddly constructed sepulcher with its twenty-some steps down into the burial chamber. Joshua was tired when he reached the spot and sat down near a well to rest. Again he caused a stir as the local inhabitants recognized him as a Jew. However, this time one of them noticed the gold medallion around his neck and was curious to see it. Their attitude immediately changed when they saw the sheik's name on the reverse of the medal. Then they couldn't do enough for him, even inviting him to their home for refreshment.

The lunch the people prepared for Joshua was light. The people were poor but generous in sharing their meager fare with this stranger, who was a friend of their relative. They asked Joshua how he came to know the sheik, and Joshua recounted for them the events of the previous day. The sheik had helped their family when they were in need, and now they were only too glad to show hospitality to a friend of the sheik's. Joshua promised to relay their kindness to the sheik when he saw him again, which he assured them would be soon. Joshua knew his path and the path of the sheik would cross again very soon and that the sheik's family would become a part of his life in the weeks to come.

"Where are you going from here?" one of the men asked Joshua.

"To Jerusalem."

"Do you have family there?" the man asked.

"No, I go on a mission of peace," Joshua answered.

"We have family in Jerusalem," the man continued. "Let me give you their names and their address. They are good people. Tell them you stayed with us and also tell them what we had for lunch. They will smile and then they will open their hearts to you. They are a big family and have done well in their lives. They are closer relatives of the sheik than our family, but we are all one, and will help you in whatever way we can. Go in peace, Joshua, and may Allah bless you."

"May Allah bless your family as well. I am grateful for your kindness," Joshua said as they parted and he walked down the road toward Jerusalem.

As Joshua wended his way along the hot, dusty road, a road traveled so many times, a flood of memories swept across his mind. The road to Bethany, which crested at the Mount of Olives, opened onto the glorious panorama that was Jerusalem with its magnificent golden-domed temple and crenellated battlements and turrets and surrounding countryside. Every place Joshua looked brought back memories, of a man and twelve companions sitting on the hillside admiring the beauty of Herod's temple, a wonder of the ancient world, and a tearful prophecy that it would all come to a bitter end because its priests failed to recognize the day of Yahweh's visitation. How vivid the memory of that briefly triumphant procession on the first Palm Sunday when the vast crowd of ordinary Jewish folk sang their hosannas to the son of David, acclaiming him as their king.

At the top of the Mount of Olives a handful of shabbily dressed Arabs was hawking postcards, handmade wooden whistles, and other cheap articles. An old man was offering a camel ride to tourists. They were gentle people trying to eke out an existence from the pennies they made, while official government tour guides were shunting their tour groups away, promising better prices and more attractive objects in "official" stores.

Joshua watched, and his face turned red with anger. Taking a batch of postcards and other objects from the children, he began offering them to the tourists at the fringe of the group. "These people are poor. They need your help," he said. "They are good people trying to earn a living. Help them."

The tour guide was furious but dared not create a scene

and just stood there while Joshua sold practically everything in sight except the old man's camel.

When the tourists left, the old man walked over to Joshua and, thanking him profusely for his courage, asked him his name. He was surprised a Jew would be so concerned.

"Things have changed lately," the old man said. "Time was when we could conduct our business undisturbed and modestly support our families on what little we made. Even Israeli soldiers would stop and buy things from us. But things are not the same now. Little things like this, mean and petty things, create anger and resentment. You would think they would understand. They were once treated this way themselves."

"Don't let it trouble you, my friend. This, too, will pass," Joshua said to him. "Don't let it poison the children's minds. Their untroubled souls are more important than a few shekels."

The children thanked Joshua, and he moved on down the slope, pausing for a few moments to contemplate the tomb of Zechariah the prophet, slain by priests right near the altar itself. The whole hillside was a vast cemetery where many a historic figure was buried, including Absalom, David's rebellious son, who was buried in a vault along the roadside below. The path Joshua trod was the same one the Son of God traveled on the first Palm Sunday, and the spot where long ago he wept over his beloved city, "Jerusalem, Jerusalem, you who have stoned the prophets and murdered those who were sent to you! How often I would have gathered you together as a hen gathers her chicks under her wings but you would not have me!" And then he cried, surprising the apostles who were not accustomed to such outbursts of emotion from their master.

As Joshua stood lost in memory, a young female Israeli soldier toting an automatic weapon over her shoulder tapped him on the arm. "Sir," she said, "could you tell me, what is this site? What is its historical significance?"

When Joshua turned toward her, she saw tears in his eyes.

"It is not a famous historic site, just a place of memories," he replied. "One day Jesus sat here on this rock looking across the valley at the temple and the beautiful city, and in prophetic vision, saw that it would one day be destroyed by Roman legions, exasperated by the people's constant rebellion."

"Are you familiar with these other sites, sir?" the girl asked Joshua.

"Yes, quite familiar," Joshua answered.

"Would you mind being our tour guide? We are all friends who have a few hours free and decided to visit historic sites but know nothing about them," the girl confided in him.

"That's all right. Not too many people know the details of their history. I would be glad to explain them to you. These sites here, except for the cemetery, are of more interest to Christians than to Jewish people. The path here going down the hillside is the path Jesus walked many times. One time when the crowds saw Jesus coming down the path on a donkey, the sight reminded them of the prophecy of Zechariah: 'Shout, O daughter of Jerusalem; Behold, your king comes to you. He is triumphant and victorious, lowly, and riding upon an ass, sitting upon a colt, the foal of an ass,' and they pulled olive branches off the trees and began to hail him as the son of David, and their king. As the procession approached the temple, the chief priests were furious at seeing their people acclaiming Jesus and demanded that it stop. It was on that day the religious leaders decided to put an end to it all. His popularity was too threatening."

Joshua's audience listened intently with eyes riveted on the walled city across the valley dominated by the Mosque of Omar. But in place of the mosque the group envisioned the ancient temple.

"On the left is the old cemetery where countless good people are buried," Joshua continued. "Following the words of the prophet Joel, many pious Jews insisted on being buried here because they believed it would be here that the souls of the just would be gathered on Judgment Day. That tomb up there to the left is where the prophet Zechariah is buried. He was murdered by the priests between the altar and the temple.

Walking down toward the bottom of the road, they reached a garden filled with ancient olive trees, some measuring over four feet in diameter. "Those trees," he said, "are over two thousand years old. If they could speak, they could tell a thousand stories.

"This is the spot where Jesus came with his apostles after celebrating the Passover for the last time. It was here he was betrayed by Judas and arrested by the temple police. They had to do this dark deed at night because the people would never have allowed it had they known.

"Over there to the left is the Valley of Hinnom, Ge-Hinnom, where human sacrifice was once offered to Moloch. King Josiah was so distraught when he witnessed the event, he ordered the place to be used from then on as a perpetual dump. Rubbish has been burning there for centuries, and the place has become a living reminder of the eternal fires of hell, and believed by some to be the very entrance to hell. No one dares go near the place after dark."

By the time Joshua finished his narrative, the group had reached the end of the path that opened onto the highway. A bus was waiting for the soldiers. They thanked Joshua for his tour, and some insisted on keeping in touch with him. A woman captain named Susan gave him her calling card and said if there was anything any of them could do for him, just to let her know. Some of her friends joshed her for being so forward; they could tell she liked Joshua. They all hoped they would meet him again on their next leave, so he could continue his guided tour.

Joshua said good-bye and started across the Kidron Valley toward Jerusalem. Entering the city through the Dung Gate, the ruins of Caiaphas' palace, he found that his memories became unusually sharp. The cold air that last night, the fires in the courtyard of the high priest, the servants standing around, and Peter and John there in their midst, and Peter's loud mouth, all filled his memory in vivid recollection. The trial before the high priest. The slap in the face by the high priest's servant. Incarceration for the night. All the sad memories of that historic evening warred in his mind.

Not far from Caiaphas' palace was the building where Jesus and the apostles celebrated the Last Supper, the Seder meal, and where, for the first time, the Eucharist had been offered.

Working his way through the city with its smells and noises and strange sights, he found himself at the Temple Mount. Gone was the temple, gone all the familiar sites. Arabs milled around the plaza in front of the grand mosque, one of the holiest shrines in Islam. Again, the same reaction on the part of Arabs toward Joshua on finding him in their midst, and even in the precincts of one of their most sacred shrines.

An elderly man approached Joshua and, seeing his apparent unawareness of the incongruity of his presence there, politely suggested that he move on before something happened. Joshua thanked him politely, telling him he had come to worship his Father. He asked if the man would accompany him into the mosque. Perplexed, the man obliged.

The inside of the holy place was covered with intricately designed ceramic tiles and columns surrounding the whole inner space. Hundreds of Persian rugs of every design and size covered the floor. Men were on their knees with hands folded and bowed to the floor as they prayed. Joshua knelt and assumed the same posture, then sat back on his heels and, resting his folded hands in his lap, closed his eyes and was soon lost in prayer.

The old man knelt near Joshua and occasionally looked over at him out of the corner of his eye. He was impressed by what he saw, and after a while just knelt back himself and watched Joshua, who was motionless for over half an hour.

After looking around admiringly at the beautiful interior, the two men walked outside.

"Young man," the Arab said, "I have never seen anyone pray like you before, and you are so young. You pray as if you really were talking to God, or perhaps listening."

"God is always close to us, and wants so very much to be part of our life. He always listens and speaks to us when we approach Him, though most people find it hard to believe that God cares," Joshua replied. "So many people pray just because they have to, not realizing what a joy it can be."

The two men stood outside the mosque, unaware that they had become an attraction, and the topic of conversation to passersby. After a while the two men parted. Joshua wandered through the streets, working his way down to the remains of the Western Wall, where he stood looking, reminiscing, and in deep thought, for the longest time.

Approaching a middle-aged man in a long black coat and beard, he attempted to strike up a conversation, but the man was too engrossed in his thoughts to notice and walked past Joshua. Joshua smiled, shaking his head in wonderment. Off to the left archeologists were working on a dig. Curious, Joshua walked along the edge of the roped-off site. The workers were friendly, as if thrilled to share their findings. Most of the workers were Jewish students from the United States, working on advanced degrees in archeology.

"Where are you from, stranger?" one of them asked

Joshua in a friendly tone, as he kept digging and scraping.

"From nearby," was Joshua's simple reply.

The men were busy conferring with one another over objects just unearthed and chatted with Joshua only between their own conversations. Joshua was content to just watch, impressed with their patience and excitement over the apparently insignificant things they uncovered, each of which had great meaning to them.

Leaving the site, Joshua walked across to the gate through which he had previously entered, and turning right, walked down the steps to the Pool of Siloam, where once a blind man had been given back his sight. Originally incorporated within the walls of the city, it was now just a shallow stream flowing from the mouth of the tunnel. Children were playing, some swimming in the cool waters of the stream. Farther downstream were lush gardens fed by the stream, in ancient times called the Garden of the Kings.

Joshua walked toward the gardens where a dozen men were working.

"Salaam aleichem!" he said to them as he approached.

"Aleichem salaam!" a few of them returned.

"A beautiful farm you have there, one of the best I have seen," Joshua told them.

"Thank you. We are fortunate here to have the stream flowing through the land. Our crops never thirst for water," one of the men replied, as Joshua walked closer.

"My name is Jakoub," the man said as he offered his hand to Joshua.

"And mine is Joshua," he returned as he shook his hand.

"It is a hot day today, Joshua. We have been working here since morning, but it is a joy to see the vegetables grow. We are fortunate," Jakoub said, mopping the sweat from his brow.

Noticing the medallion around Joshua's neck, the Arab remarked, "That medallion you have around your neck, I have seen only a few others like it, specially made by my uncle, Sheik Ibrahim."

Joshua smiled. Everything was unfolding as planned. "Yes, this was made by your uncle. He gave it to me yesterday," Joshua told him.

"May I see it?" the gardener asked.

"Yes," Joshua said, as he removed it from his neck and held it out to Jakoub.

It was the same simply designed medal Jakoub had seen before, given by his uncle to a few extraordinary people for whom he felt profound gratitude.

"You must be a very special person, Joshua, for the sheik to honor you the way he did. And I can tell you are not one of us, so my uncle paid you a rare honor. And did you eat with the sheik's family?"

"I did, and I stopped at your cousin's home in Bethany as well. They offered me some of the pepper sauce the sheik had given them. I never tasted anything so hot," Joshua replied, and went on to describe the meal.

Jakoub laughed loudly and said, "Just like uncle. He makes that pepper sauce himself and gives jars to all the family. Most of us can't eat it, it's so hot. The sheik is like a father to all of us. I am glad you found your way to my home. As the sheik's nephew, you do me honor by visiting here. I also am in your debt for whatever kindness you showed my uncle. These are all my relatives here working with me. I will introduce them to you. We are almost finished for the day and will be leaving shortly. You must come home with me and tell me why you have come. We will help you in whatever way we can."

As the men picked up their tools and came together before starting home, Jakoub introduced them to Joshua. They, too, recognized the medallion, but discreetly waited until later to question Jakoub about it.

CHAPTER 3

J AKOUB'S FAMILY was large. He and his wife Shareen had three daughters and five sons. Four of them were married: two living nearby and two living in Nazareth. The ones living nearby were home visiting. Their other children ranged from fourteen to eight. Their house was a well-built rambling home of stone and stucco, with enough space to create a comfortable atmosphere.

On entering the house, Jakoub stunned everyone as he introduced Joshua. They just were not accustomed to their father bringing a Jew into the house, and what was even more shocking, introducing him as a friend. Once Jakoub had Joshua tell them the story behind the medallion, however, everyone relaxed, and the evening proceeded happily.

It was cool that night, so the family decided to eat outside in the courtyard. The meal, while painstakingly prepared, was not fancy, but tastefully put together from meats and vegetables grown and raised on their modest farm.

Joshua relished the meal as was clear from his expressions, and congratulated Jakoub on the excellent wine he had produced from local grapes. He was hungry after the day's journey and was grateful for this family's kindness to a stranger who was not even one of their own.

After supper, which lasted until past midnight, the family

scattered. Jakoub took Joshua aside, and the two of them talked far into the night.

"Joshua, you are an unusual man," Jakoub said, once they were alone. "I watched you at table tonight. You talked to each one of the family; even the little children you treated with respect. They wanted very much for you to stay over so they could spend time with you in the morning. I trust you will honor our family by sleeping here with us."

"It is I who am honored," Joshua replied. "Yes, I would like that. My work is finished for the day, so I would be only too happy to stay with you."

"Joshua, you mentioned you had a purpose in being here," Jakoub continued. "May I ask what it might be, because, out of loyalty to the sheik, I would like to place myself and my family at your service."

"It is sad seeing all the violence and hatred that infects our people's lives," Joshua started by saying. "Everyone wants peace, but no one knows where to start or whom to trust, and people are afraid not to hate, for fear of letting down their defenses. I would like to reach out and make friends with good families on both sides and, in time, bring them all together in a special closely knit community of Jewish and Arab families."

"That's a dangerous goal, Joshua. You'll be lucky not to be assassinated, like some of our noblest people who tried to reach out and make friends with Jews. Fanatics looked upon them as traitors and informers," Jakoub responded.

"I know that, but I am not afraid, my friend," Joshua responded calmly. "God's work cannot be abandoned because of fear of fanatics. Evil people can only kill the body. They cannot touch the soul, and that is what counts. Your family is a good family, Jakoub, and you could be a powerful instrument of Allah in assisting in this work. It will ultimately be successful and will bring God's peace to your people, and to all people. There are many Jewish people of goodwill who will also be willing to sacrifice them-

selves to bring peace to this troubled land. Working together, we will be able to forge a powerful alliance that can create the pressure needed to promote peace. Will you work
with me?"

"I have no choice, Joshua. The sheik has committed his
whole tribe to support you. I will be by your side, and my
family will as well," Jakoub assured.

The next morning before breakfast Joshua spent time
with the children, telling them stories and playing tricks
that kept them spellbound. After breakfast, he thanked the
family for their warm hospitality and departed.

Walking across town, he ended up in the business section
of Jerusalem and stopped at Ben-Yehuda Street, a quiet
oasis in the midst of all the downtown hubbub. People
were sitting around tables neatly placed along the sidewalks
on both sides of the street, on which no vehicles were
allowed.

Joshua sat down at one of the tables and ordered coffee.
Two Israeli soldiers on patrol were casually sipping coffee at
the next table and unobtrusively keeping an eye on everything that happened on the street.

One of them recognized Joshua from seeing him wandering around the day before and started a conversation with
him.

"You really get around, young man," the soldier mentioned casually, though gently prying for information. "It
isn't every day you see a Jew wandering in the vicinity of
the mosque, much less stopping in to pray. I noticed you up
on the Temple Mount yesterday near the mosque. Are you
a tourist on holiday?"

"Yes, I suppose you might say that. I enjoy visiting all
the beautiful sites," Joshua responded in friendly fashion.

"I think some of my friends bumped into you on the hill
yesterday while they were touring the sites around the old
cemetery," the other soldier remarked. "They were quite
impressed with your description of the sites over there."

Joshua laughed and thanked him for the compliment.

"If you are going to be around later this afternoon, you may see them. They're scheduled to patrol here on the next shift. They'll be glad to see you," the same soldier said, rising from the table with his buddy and walking off with automatic rifles slung over their shoulders.

As they left, Joshua spotted two men on the opposite side of the street discreetly turning their backs as the soldiers rose and turned in their direction. Joshua had seen them, the same two men, the day before on the Temple Mount. They reminded him of the scribes' and Pharisees' spies of old. He was to see these men and others like them more and more in the days to come. They were certainly not tourists or businessmen or even casual townsfolk strolling for exercise. They were men with a purpose, and with his uncanny sense of people, Joshua knew only too well that that purpose was dark and threatening.

Finishing his coffee, he rose and walked down the street, admiring objects in store windows all along the way. At the corner he turned up the street, then crossed over, discreetly looking back to see if he was being followed. The same two men were not far behind, appearing to be window-shopping.

Joshua slipped around the next corner and disappeared. It would serve no good purpose, he thought, to let his life become an open book to that kind of people. His mission was too important . . . and too easily misunderstood.

For a person who was supposedly a stranger in the city, Joshua knew exactly whom he wanted to see and where they lived. Continuing on his jaunt, he worked his way to the government office buildings and sat on a bench nearby. A middle-aged man left the building and approached the bench where Joshua was sitting.

"Daniel, I have something to discuss with you," Joshua said as the man was passing the bench. "You are on your way to the parking lot. Do not drive your car today. It is not safe."

The man looked at Joshua as if he were crazy.

"Why are you telling me this, and how do you know? And how do you know my name?" the man asked in rapid succession.

"You are a good man, Daniel, and your vision of peace is upsetting people who are bent on evil. You are frustrating their schemes."

"Who are you?" Daniel asked.

"My name is Joshua, and I would like to work with you on your plan for peace," Joshua answered simply.

"Thank you, but I hardly know you. I do appreciate your interest. We shall see," the man said.

"I will be around. We will find each other," Joshua said, then walked off.

Toward evening Joshua found himself back on Ben-Yehuda Street, and just as the soldiers told him earlier in the day, found his friends on duty patrolling the street. They immediately recognized him walking up the street, but being on duty were not as sociable as the day before.

"Joshua, our tour guide!" one of them exclaimed. They both greeted him warmly, chatted briefly, telling him how much they enjoyed his tour.

"If you are going to be here after we finish our duty," one of them said, "some of our friends are meeting us and we can spend some time together. We are not supposed to fraternize while we are on patrol."

"I understand. That would be nice," Joshua replied. "Yes, I will be here, and will enjoy spending time with you."

It was cool later in the evening. The street was filled with visitors sitting at tables all along the street, sipping a variety of coffees and other drinks and eating Greek pastries, creating a happy, friendly atmosphere. The two soldiers came by as they promised and soon afterward their comrades, six in all besides Joshua, including the colonel, Aaron Bessmer, a physicist, and the captain, Susan Horowitz.

They were all glad to see him. After ordering their coffee and pastries, they sat back and jumped into their conversation. Aaron began, "Joshua, I heard about your escapade this afternoon. You have been in town only a day and you have already got yourself into the thick of things. We had to send a bomb squad to Daniel Sharon's car. Do you realize you actually saved his life?"

Joshua answered simply, "Yes, I could see he was walking into trouble. I am impressed with the efficiency of your intelligence and how you put all the pieces together."

Aaron laughed. "There's not much happens here we don't know about. Our existence depends on it."

"How did you know his car was booby-trapped?" Aaron asked, half as a friendly question and half as part of an investigation.

"Some things I just know," Joshua answered. "As soon as the man walked toward me I could see the danger he was in. I knew he was a good man, so I felt I should warn him."

"Had someone told you about the bomb?" Aaron asked.

"No, I wasn't aware of anything until that moment. But when I saw the man, I knew clearly," Joshua replied.

The captain interrupted. "Aaron, I'm surprised at you. You are interrogating our friend as if he were a suspect. We are grateful, Joshua, you saved our friend's life."

"I've known of Daniel and his family for a long time," Joshua said. "What he is trying to accomplish is admirable, but he exposes himself to risk from people who do not want peace and are threatened by people working together."

"Joshua, I am amazed you are so familiar with what's happening around here," Susan said.

"Anyone who is concerned should be vitally interested in those who are making an effort to bring peace to our troubled land," Joshua replied. "With all the blessings God has showered on this land, people still have never learned to respect one another as God's children. That is the great evil."

"Well, I don't think God has anything to do with it," one of the others named Nathan interjected. "In fact, it's the religious people who cause much of the problem. I gave up religion myself precisely because of all the hypocrisy. I feel if there is a God, He has to love everybody. It is stupid to think that God would create a race of people and then pick sides and show favorites. He would want them all to get along. During the wars chaplains on both sides prayed that God would help them destroy the enemy. It doesn't make sense. Everyone expects God to be on their side while they kill one another. That has to be offensive to God if He's real."

Susan agreed. "I don't share your lack of faith. I still believe in God," she said, "but I've only come across one rabbi who made sense. He seemed to have faced all these issues honestly himself, and discussed them freely with the congregation. He used to be Orthodox but they kicked him out. I heard him in a Reform synagogue in Tel Aviv. He really renewed my faith in God."

Aaron listened intently to the other two and watched Joshua's reaction. He was just listening. "My family's been here a long time," Aaron said. "Long before all the trouble started. In fact, for years my folks were partners with an Arab family in a business venture. We are still friends, but we had to dissolve the partnership because people made it so difficult to operate. My sister Rebecca is married to one of their family, and we all get along famously."

"My family is Orthodox," one of the others named Samuel contributed. "They feel that we are still God's chosen people, and should be totally separated from the Arabs. In fact they won't feel comfortable until all the Arabs are driven out of the land. They just don't feel good about others living in their community."

"That's really racist," Susan said sharply.

"It may be racist, but that's the way they feel," Samuel retorted. "Their families have seen a lot of persecution and injustice in their day. Besides that, they feel God gave them this land and it rightfully belongs to them."

"How is that any different from Hitler with his idea of the pure Aryan race?" Aaron added.

"Come now, Aaron, there's a big difference between the two," Samuel shot back.

"Yeah, we use God to justify it," Aaron said bitterly. "I have a problem with the religious approach to our troubles. I'm not religious, but I know our history well, and I believe God had a purpose when He called Abraham and when He led our people out of Egypt, and sent prophets to guide them. There was an objective to their being isolated in this land, so God could prepare them for something special. For many centuries God was involved with them, as our religious books record. But then it ended. The prophecies ended. Our Bible ended. It is as if what God intended was accomplished. For people who say that God's chosen purpose is still continuing among us, I fail to see it. Where is the evidence?"

"What do you think, Joshua?" Susan asked. "You've been sitting there thinking deeply during all this exchange."

"We are still God's chosen people," Joshua responded, "but times change and needs change. When a people are chosen by God, they are chosen for a reason, as Aaron indicated so beautifully. They gave to the world a whole new civilization that they can still affect if they so choose, or they can live in the ancient past and withdraw from modern life as some do. But the people will always be special to God and have a special mission. All God's children are special for different reasons. For one people to feel that they are the only ones loved by God is not good. God loves all His children. The situation here in our land is different now from what it was in the distant past, and all the people here must learn not to cut themselves off from each other, or look upon the others as intruders, but to be responsible for one another, and to care for one another, and to get along as one nation. It is the only way life can exist in this land. Any other way is self-destructive and offensive to God."

"Well put!" a quiet fellow named Reuben chimed in.

"Joshua," Susan started, "tell us something about yourself. Where are you from? And what do you do?"

"I was born not far from here, in Bethlehem," Joshua answered casually. "I live simply. I am deeply concerned about our inability as a people to solve the problems we face, and I walk from place to place trying to encourage people to think differently."

"Like what, for example?" Aaron asked.

"Like what we were talking about before and about what you said, Aaron," Joshua replied. "It is a fact that Arabs and Jews share this land. It is not that one is good and the other evil. Each is trying to live life in peace. Many good people live here but feel threatened by the other, and not without cause. There has been much hurt and pain inflicted by both sides. Neither is innocent, so neither should stand self-righteous as if their hands are unbloodied. The meanness and pettiness has to stop, and we have to cut a new road, a new path of decency and tolerance and kindness to one another. It will not be simple, nor will it bear fruit immediately. Just as it took time for the hatred to take root and spread, so it will take time for the kindness to take root. But with patience and a willingness to forgive, in time the atmosphere will change. I go from place to place sowing the seeds of kindness and goodwill. Some listen and respond. Some resist. But with patience we will succeed."

"You seem so confident and so casual about it, Joshua," Susan commented.

"It is the only way to be," Joshua replied. "A program like this, by its very nature, is a long, tedious process. It has to be the work of a lifetime, not of a day. We may not reap the fruit tomorrow, but our children will live to enjoy the fruits of peace and goodwill. I am confident it will succeed, so I am patient."

"You talk to Arabs, too?" Reuben asked.

"Yes. How can we solve the problems if we do not talk to them?" Joshua answered.

"Aren't you afraid?" Reuben continued.

"We can't afford to be afraid when important work has to be done," Joshua rejoined. "It is God's work and God takes care of those who work with Him. We can never be afraid. It is only those who can kill the soul we should fear."

It was not just talk, it was the way Joshua lived. His Father was always real to him, so he walked through danger unafraid.

"Joshua, that medal around your neck," Susan noted. "It is beautiful. Where did you get it, if I may ask?"

Taking off the medallion, Joshua handed it to her. Turning it over, she read the back of the medallion, "'Sheik Ibrahim Saud.' You know him?" she asked, shocked.

"I met him one night and helped his family when they were hurting," Joshua answered. "He was grateful and gave me the medallion as a gift."

"You must have done him a huge favor for him to give you this. He has committed his whole family to you. That man is like Abraham. He has family everywhere. It seems half of Jerusalem is related to him. He is one powerful friend to have, Joshua, I hope you realize that," Susan assured him, returning the medallion.

"We have been trying for years to get him to work with us, but he has always been wary of our intentions," Aaron said.

"What kind of work, Aaron?" Joshua asked.

"A group of us," Aaron replied, "have been trying discreetly to reach out to certain decent Arab families and form an alliance of like-minded people to create a healthier atmosphere in our country. Daniel Sharon is one of us. That's why they tried to kill him. There is no reason why we can't all work together and do things together, socially and in other ways. The sheik would be a great help, but for some reason he stays aloof. Yet he's a good man, a decent person."

"That is a noble goal," Joshua agreed. "As I wander around I will gather those who are interested. It is something we can all work on together."

"How long do you think it will take you to gather your friends, Joshua?" Aaron asked.

"Give me a few days," Joshua answered.

"Good. Then we will meet here in three days, same time," Aaron said decisively, and everyone assented.

CHAPTER 4

THE NEXT three days Joshua wandered around the city and its environs, meeting people, searching out those who would be open to his message of peace. On the third day he stopped at the Church of the Holy Sepulcher, the traditional site of Calvary and the Tomb. It was now under the protection of various ecclesiastical groups who were constantly feuding for control of the sacred site.

When Joshua arrived at the church, the tomb was open to view but Calvary was encased in marble walls which made the site of the Crucifixion inaccessible except for a foot-wide hole at the top of the marble staircase, through which a pilgrim could reach down and touch the ground which was Calvary.

Approaching the tomb, around which a small crowd was standing, Joshua waited in line for his turn to enter. Just as his turn came, it was time for the scheduled change of jurisdiction. The Catholic Franciscans were guarding the site during the day. Now it was being turned over to Greek Orthodox. Something occurred between the two groups that occasioned a heated discussion. They had almost reached the point of fisticuffs as Joshua was entering and accidentally bumped into him, shoving him into the barricade, where he lost his balance and fell.

Angered, Joshua arose, and looking at the group of them

asked them pointedly, "Are you people Christians or hood-lums? If you can't conduct yourselves with dignity and charity, it would be better to turn the site over to heathens. They would show more respect."

Both groups were highly incensed at the stinging indict-ment and physically ushered Joshua out of the shrine, telling him that if he couldn't come with a better attitude, he should stay away from this sacred place. On this, at least, they could agree.

An old Franciscan friar with white beard and rustic walk-ing stick saw what had happened and walked over to Joshua.

"I am sorry, my son," the old priest said to him. "It is a shame priests can't conduct themselves with charity. They are a disgrace and a scandal. This has been going on for centuries, and it seems it will never end."

"Religion is a game with these people," Joshua said, "and competition their liturgy. They are in love with their churches and their traditions, not God. Their rituals are hollow praise, and God would turn a deaf ear were it not for the simple faith of pious people who come here with rever-ence. It would be better if these buildings were never built, so people could be inspired by the uncluttered simplicity of the sites themselves."

"Sit down here, young man, and talk to me," the old priest said as he sat down on the bench near the wall. "My name is Father Ambrose Boyd. What is your name?"

"My name is Joshua," he responded.

"Don't be offended by what happened," the priest said by way of apology. "We are not all that way. Most of the priests who come here are pious men completely dedicated to these shrines. A few are feisty, and they cause all the trouble. They are an embarrassment to our community. I came here years ago in an attempt to sow seeds of peace in this troubled land. It has been a difficult road. Now I am old and see more meanness and hatred than ever."

"I have come for that same reason," Joshua said. "Gather your friends together and work with me. Together we will accomplish much."

"I have all kinds of strange friends," the priest said, "even Orthodox priests like the ones in there. They are not all political like those fellows. Some are decent men, though they stay more with their own, and don't mingle. We meet regularly and pray together, even in our Lord's own language. I have other friends who are Arab and Jewish Christians, a quiet little group. These are the best of all, the cream. I would like you to meet them sometime."

"I would like to. We must all work together if there is to be peace," Joshua told the priest.

"I am old. My work is done," the priest complained.

"Your work is not done, Father. The best is yet to come," Joshua reassured him.

"What can I do?" he asked Joshua.

"Keep preaching your message of peace," Joshua told him. "Soon we will all come together and show the world how beautiful it is for brothers and sisters to work in harmony."

"I must go and take a rest; I tire easily. Thank you for taking the time to talk with me, young man. I enjoyed it very much," Father Ambrose said. Then he rose and said, "Good-bye."

"We will meet again, Father," Joshua responded.

On the afternoon of the third day Joshua left the city for Bethlehem, just a few miles away. As it was late in the day, he did not walk the whole way to Bethlehem, but slept in the hills that night in a grove of olive trees, with the roots of a tree as his pillow. The canteen given to him by the Arab boy came in good stead, as the days were hot and in the hills there was no water.

The next day, Joshua reached Bethlehem. The town

proper was, as then, small, with a massive shrine church hovering over the traditional site commemorating Jesus' birth two thousand years ago, and surrounded by Orthodox and Catholic convents. A vast square in front of the entrance seemed to shrink the small portal, intentionally designed that way to keep hostile soldiers from riding their horses into the sacred shrine.

The area surrounding Bethlehem was no longer a little hamlet out in the hills. It had become a sprawling community extending far beyond its original boundaries and home to over a hundred and fifty thousand people, mostly Arabs. There was a university in the village now, run by Christian Brothers, educating not just Christians living in the area but Muslims as well. Christian Arabs and Muslims had lived together in peace in this community for decades.

Joshua walked through the town, talking casually to people he met along the way, paying special attention as always to the little children.

As he was sitting in the village square around noon, a tall, thin man approached him, and in friendly manner introduced himself. "My name is Naim," he said, with a broad smile that betrayed a perfect set of white teeth. He held out his hand for Joshua to shake.

"I am Joshua," Joshua responded, as the two men shook hands.

"I have a little business here," Naim said. "We carve wooden figurines out of olive wood. Your face looks very much like one of our carvings, so I had to say hello to you."

"I passed your store. You have good people working for you," Joshua said.

"Thank you," Naim replied. "Yes, we try to hire honest people. They are all Arabs, some Christians, a number of Muslims. They work well together."

"That's the way it should be," Joshua remarked. "You have made a good contribution to peace."

"I try to do my little part," Naim answered with a touch

of pride. "I know it is not much, but it shows how people can work together. They all live here in the village or roundabout and are good neighbors to one another. We have had peaceful relations here for a long time. Some of our people used to be members of the Knesset. Lately, however, relations are strained; we feel a kinship and a loyalty to our brothers who are hurting in other areas of the country. It didn't used to be that way, but each government is different and treats the Arab population differently. Some day, perhaps, some day, we will learn to respect one another."

Joshua told the man of his concerns, and before they finished speaking, Joshua had another follower, glad to be part of his undertaking. The man liked Joshua and invited him to stay at his house and meet his family, which he did.

The next day, as Joshua was walking through the village, he noticed the two men who had been following him in Jerusalem now tailing him through the streets of Bethlehem. He walked past the town, out into the countryside, and wandered through the Shepherds' Field. Sheep and goats had grazed there for thousands of years. Their shepherds had never been well treated by polite society. In fact, they were despised by religious people for not keeping the law.

Joshua thought of the events of so long ago when angels appeared to shepherds telling them of Jesus' birth. Shepherds were the first to show the newborn honor, the first to welcome him. Others had no room for him, or showed no interest. The walk through the hillside held, perhaps, the most tender of memories for Joshua. Joseph had tried so hard to make events surrounding the birth joyful and comfortable, but all he could find was a smelly stable. To Joshua, things like that were unimportant.

*   *   *

Leaving the field, Joshua began his trip back to Jerusalem. That night he met his friends at the cafe on Ben-Yehuda Street. They were dressed in ordinary clothes and were glad to see him.

"We haven't seen you around, Joshua," Susan began. "I take it you have been busy."

"Yes, there was much to be done, and much has been accomplished," he replied. "One of the details I thought important was a place for us to meet. The manager of the Seven Arches is very enthused about our work and offered to let us use their facilities for meetings."

Aaron was surprised, but delighted. He then brought the group up-to-date on their accomplishments so far. Daniel Sharon wanted Aaron to thank Joshua for saving his life and said he would thank him personally when he met him. He then explained that their network of friends was still small but excited about the prospect of doing something tangible that would have some positive effect on the community. They were all happy about Joshua's contacts with Arab people who were interested in working with them to promote peace.

Joshua told them of the people he had met and of their willingness to come to a meeting.

"Joshua," Samuel said in an almost unbelieving tone, "how could you possibly have persuaded those Arabs to agree to come to a meeting, something we have tried in vain to do for months, even with our best show of goodwill?"

Joshua smiled and replied, "Perhaps it is due to their allegiance to the sheik. Whatever, they are committed to work with us and are waiting for us to set the date."

"Aaron," Susan said, "I think we should tell Joshua about his shadows, or we may all end up with a surprise we can't handle."

"Joshua," Aaron said, "I don't know how to tell you this, but you are being followed by intelligence people. They work on their own, and are totally independent of us. We have no control over their activities. You will really have to be careful."

"I realize that already," Joshua replied, not too terribly concerned. "I have seen them on a number of occasions. It is a problem I have always had. We need not worry. This mission will not fail. What we are doing is God's work."

"I wish I had your confidence," Nathan interjected. "Every attempt in the past to get Arabs and Jews to work together has come to a miserable end. There are just too many people whose interest it is to keep the two sides enemies." Nathan was a young man in his early twenties, bright and quick-witted, with curly brown hair and an infectious laugh.

"We have to trust God to be with us," Joshua replied. "Prayer would help. With our Father's help, it is possible. Without Him it won't succeed."

The group decided that they should work out the details of their first meeting at the Seven Arches Hotel. Joshua told them to expect close to thirty Arabs for that meeting. These thirty Arabs were willing to test the waters at the first meeting, and then to commit themselves and their families, if they felt comfortable after this meeting. The date was set for the next week, depending upon available space, which Joshua assured them would be no problem. The group then broke up, with Aaron taking Joshua to his house to meet his family.

Aaron's family lived in a well-to-do section of town, in the hills outside the city. Their house was not large but pleasingly designed, and well-appointed inside. Aaron's wife, Esther, was tall, with long, straight black hair, and dark blue eyes, appearing at times to be almost violet. Her smooth olive complexion made her look far too young to be the mother of three children.

Esther welcomed Joshua warmly and told her husband to

bring him into the kitchen. She was preparing food for the next day.

"I am thrilled to meet you, Joshua," Esther said as they entered the kitchen. "You are all Aaron has been talking about since the day he met you. You certainly made an impression on him. He doesn't usually fuss over people."

"Well, now you can see for yourself, I am just a simple man," Joshua answered.

"Not so simple, Joshua. There is something about you that made me take notice as soon as you walked in," Esther told him. "You have such a tranquil bearing."

"Thank you, you flatter me," Joshua replied.

"Joshua, how about a glass of homemade wine, the best in the country?" Aaron boasted as he offered his guest a glass.

"Sounds good. Homemade is always the best. It's alive," Joshua responded, picking up the glass Aaron had poured for him. Aaron poured a glass for his wife, and for the children and himself, then they saluted "L'chayim" to one another.

"Esther, this man is absolutely amazing," Aaron said, as soon as he swallowed his first mouthful. "Do you know what he has done?"

"I don't have the slightest idea," Esther replied.

"He got a whole group of important Arabs to join with us in our movement," Aaron told her. "Something we haven't been able to do in over two years of hard work." Then, turning to Joshua, he asked, "How did you ever do it?"

"Oh, I merely hypnotized them. Then, when they were completely in my power, I told them they had to come. It was so simple," Joshua said flippantly.

"Come, now. You know it wasn't an easy task," Aaron pressed him. "What did you say to them?"

"Everyone wants to live in peace, so I just convinced them that if they really cared, they had to make their own contribution to peace, not just wish it," Joshua answered simply.

"When we get them all together, how shall we handle it? That's going to be the touchy part," Aaron said, concerned.

"Let me handle the groups. I can guide them gently and they won't be suspicious of me," Joshua offered.

"Sounds like it might work. They trust you already and will be more willing to listen to you than to any of us. Do you think the sheik will come?"

"I think he might come for the first meeting out of courtesy. Then, if he feels comfortable, he will bring others to future meetings," Joshua said confidently.

One of the children, three-year-old Mirza, had worked her way over to Joshua and asked if she could sit on his lap. She was round-faced, with big, black eyes. Joshua chuckled and said he would be thrilled if she would. Climbing up, she wiggled her way into his lap and sat there with a look of pride, as Joshua cradled her in his arms. Her two brothers laughed, so she stuck out her tongue at them. Her brothers, Moishe, a skinny, nervous eleven-year-old, and David, a playful, happy seven-year-old, were always in trouble for teasing their baby sister, who could do no wrong. This time they really asked for it when David made the wise remark, "Moishe, she likes Joshua so much, maybe we'll be lucky and he'll kidnap her."

"David, I hate you, I hate you," was their sister's immediate response.

Joshua assured her with a hug that he would never do such a thing and that he would send a special angel down from heaven just to protect her, so that no one would ever harm her.

David was peremptorily shipped off to his room and told to get ready for bed. Not long afterward the other children followed, which left Aaron and Esther in peace with Joshua. They stayed up late sharing thoughts they never imagined they could share with anyone.

"Joshua, if I am not being personal, where do you sleep?" Aaron asked almost apologetically.

"Usually out in the hills, where it is quiet, and I can just lie under the trees in an olive grove and look up into the sky. It is peaceful. On cool nights, I light a fire and sit and think, and talk to my Father, then fall asleep."

"You really feel close to God, don't you?" Esther asked.

"Yes, He is always close by. I draw my strength from Him and also my vision. He is the reason for my confidence in the future," he responded.

"Joshua," Aaron said, "I had the strangest feeling the first day we met, when you were describing the sites across the Kidron, that you had personally witnessed what you were narrating. I immediately felt a kinship with you and knew I could trust you."

"These places have always been dear to me, every stone and every path, and every brook. They should be precious to every child of Israel," Joshua replied. "Yahweh's presence has always hovered over this city, and everyone, Jew and Arab, should feel it is their home, and not a place of endless conflict, like it is."

"I mentioned earlier that my sister is married to an Arab," Aaron said. "His family has lived here for generations. They are really saintly people and often talk about feeling the presence of God in this city. It is a real spiritual home to them.

"Joshua, if you like, you are more than welcome to stay here with our family, rather than sleep out in the hills at night," Aaron said to him.

"Your offer is generous," said Joshua, "but it is better that I stay alone. It is the way I have always been, and I feel at home under the stars. My Father feels very close when I'm alone."

It was late when they retired. Bringing an extra towel to Joshua's room, Aaron rapped on the door, impulsively opening it, and caught Joshua kneeling near the window wrapped in prayer, unaware that Aaron had even entered the room.

Aaron left the towel on the chair nearby and quietly withdrew, with the image burnt into his thoughts.

CHAPTER **5**

EVERYONE ROSE early the next morning. Aaron had to be at the office for a special briefing, so breakfast was rushed. After breakfast, Joshua left and continued on his way. He wanted to meet the old Franciscan priest who was so kind to him earlier that week. The man's sincerity and wide circle of friends could be a great asset in the present venture.

Joshua met him in the same place as before. It seemed the priest spent much of his time of late in the precincts of the sacred shrine, meditating on the life of Jesus and the ways of God, and trying to show kindness to pilgrims of whatever race or belief.

"Father Ambrose, I was hoping I would find you here," Joshua said as he met the old priest sitting on a chair meditating. "I have been thinking much about you since our last visit. We are planning a meeting at the Seven Arches and we would like very much for you to come with your many friends. All your prayer and hard work is coming to fruition. I hope you can make it."

The old priest was thrilled. He could see that his work was not ended. He did still have a purpose. His brown eyes twinkled with a new life. "My son, I am glad you did not forget me. I have been praying for you since your unfortunate visit here last week. I will be happy to come to your meeting. I will contact all my friends. I am sure they will want to come as well."

The two men went over to the site of the tomb, and the priest escorted Joshua inside, explaining important information about the history and archeology through the centuries. Joshua was indeed impressed, and the priest was delighted he could provide him with a personal tour.

With almost a week before the meeting at the Seven Arches, Joshua decided to leave Jerusalem and wander far up north, to Tabor and Nazareth and Cana on his way to Capernaum, and on his return trip to the shrine to the prophet Elijah on Mount Carmel. Nain, as in days of old, was still sparse—simple houses with round stone ovens dotting the field just off the highway. A mournful dirge and the image of a brokenhearted mother still sparked memories . . . memories of a man, once dead, now stretching his arms to the heavens. The long distance of time seemed to have little effect in erasing the vivid recollections so full of meaning.

Tabor loomed high over the village.

Reaching the top of Tabor, Joshua walked the rocky perimeter, surveying the valley that surrounded the huge rock that thrust seemingly to the clouds. Here was a perfect vantage point to scan massive military operations forming far below. Long ago, Peter, James, and John were lifted from their senses in seeing Jesus conferring with Moses and Elijah. Overwhelmed, Peter offered to build a shrine to commemorate the event.

As Joshua walked the hilltop, lost in memory, two reconnaissance jets zoomed overhead.

Nazareth was no longer the little village of previous times. It was now a major city in the north with a mixed population of mostly Muslims, with Catholics, Orthodox, and various Protestant groups, and a large Jewish community, all living in their own sections of town. Joshua's memories as he walked into the city were mixed. His previous visit here had been, he thought, his last. The townsfolk had tried to kill him. But it had not always been that way. There were pleasant memories, too, of childhood and his youthful years. He walked past the spot where once his house stood, no longer there. Sights, sounds, and smells of old filled his senses as he remembered a thousand details of life so long ago. Walking down the street he could see his mother on her way to the well from which people were even now drawing water. He stopped to drink the cool, fresh water he once drank daily, and drew so often for his mother who, it seemed, was always working, or worrying about him. Memories of his foster father's workshop filled his mind, and the many hours spent there helping him, and the sad day when Joseph died, leaving him and his mother all alone. Tender memories, so vivid!

The new basilica dedicated to the coming of the Word of God in human flesh, a massive structure built to accommodate huge crowds, dominated the city. Underneath in the crypt was the reason for the building. There, dramatically displayed for pilgrims to see, were remains of the home where Mary lived when the angel appeared to her, and next to it a small shrine built by the earliest Christians, with the telltale red cross marked on the wall, and the words in Greek, "This shrine was built to honor Mary, the Mother of Jesus, by her family and friends." On another slab of stone from the earliest Christian period were marked the words, "Jesus, Son of God."

Joshua tried in his imagination to strip away the stone, the glass, and the steel and picture the scene as it had been, as he remembered it so well. It was a simple house, like so many others in the village. His grandmother and grandfather, a learned priest, lived there and were always thrilled when he came to visit them, bringing them presents he had just made—a chair or a bench or a small cabinet. His mother seemed so young at the time, just a child herself, so full of laughter and joy, in spite of the harshness of life and the priest's prophecy that her life would be pierced by seven swords. He remembered being in love with his mother. She was the most beautiful woman he had ever seen. His Father couldn't have given him a better mother, though she worried about him too much, and to his child's way of thinking, was overly protective. His foster father, Joseph, was a good match. His love for Miriam was so tender, bordering almost on veneration. He knew she was special to God; she was special to him as well. He treated her accordingly.

As Joshua was pondering all these memories, a nun walked past with a group of Arab children, explaining to them the story of the place, which roused Joshua from his reveries.

Exiting the building, he wandered through the town. It was far different from the way he remembered it. Walking back down the street to the well, he sat down on the stone ledge that flanked the fountain, as if waiting for someone.

After a few minutes, a man in his early forties passed. Joshua caught his eye, and nonchalantly said, "Shalom." The man returned the greeting, and something made him stop and walk over to Joshua.

"You seem so at home sitting here, yet I can tell you are a stranger. It is as if I should know you, but I don't. May I ask your name, sir?" the man said to Joshua.

"Yes, my name is Joshua. I'm just traveling and stopped for a rest. May I ask your name?"

"My name is Samuel."

"That's a good name. Great men carried that name," Joshua responded.

"Yes, I know. I try to live up to it," the man returned.

"The mood is so peaceful today. The air is quiet, the breeze so gentle. It is too bad people can't have the same peace inside. It would make for a much better world," Joshua said.

"I have lived here all my life and have never known peace," Samuel replied. "It seems someone is always stirring up trouble. If they don't have a reason, they invent one. I would give anything to see peace in our country."

"Samuel, follow me and I will lead you to peace," Joshua said, to the man's surprise.

"Follow you? Follow you where?" Samuel asked, confused.

"I have come to bring peace, and God's help will make it possible. Find your friends and bring them to me, and I will lead you to peaceful waters," Joshua continued.

"You are a strange man, Joshua. But there is something about you that commands my respect," Samuel answered. "Where will we find you?"

"I will wait here for you," Joshua told him.

It was not long before the man returned with his friends, over a dozen of them, all curious to meet this strange man.

After they had all been introduced to Joshua, they walked to a quiet area, and Joshua spoke to them. "The reason the world has no peace is that people have no peace inside themselves. How can people give peace if they have not found peace themselves? Peace means disciplining what is unruly and harmful within ourselves. It means overlooking hurt and insult and forgiving those who offend you. It means reaching out to God and allowing Him into your soul, where He can become your friend. When God is within you, then you will have peace. Bringing peace to the world means bringing God into the hearts of others. It cannot be otherwise. You cannot have peace without God. You are His children, and you will always be troubled as long as you are orphaned from God. I have come to help you find your heavenly Father."

The men listened intently, not knowing what to think. They had never heard a man talk like this before. He was different, yet his words touched their hearts deeply, and they were moved.

"We will follow you, sir," one of them said, and to a man the others agreed. "Where will we meet with you?"

"In Jerusalem," Joshua replied. "On the Mount of Olives, next Wednesday evening at seven o'clock. There will be others, good people, all searching for peace."

"I will be there," Samuel promised, "and the others as well. Shalom."

"Shalom," Joshua returned. And they departed.

Joshua walked through town, toward the spot where the ancient synagogue stood, the place where he had worshiped as a child and a young man, the place where he learned his lessons about God and the Torah, and the history of his people. At the spot, now covered over with tons of debris and a modern building, he stood and remembered his last visit. He had just begun his public ministry, filled with enthusiasm. Word had gotten back to Nazareth that he had been preaching and working miracles in Jerusalem, and the townsfolk were jealous. On his return, his neighbors invited him to speak in the synagogue one Saturday.

It was with fear and trepidation that he started reading the scroll that was handed him: "The spirit of the Lord God is upon me; because the Lord has anointed me to bring good news to the humble; He has sent me to bind up the brokenhearted, to proclaim liberty to captives, sight to the blind; to proclaim the year of the Lord's favor, and the day of recompense from our God."

Putting down the scroll, he looked across the packed meeting room and quietly announced, "This day, this prophecy has been fulfilled in your very sight. No doubt you will say to me, physician, cure yourself. Work here among your own the miracles we heard you have been working for others. And I cannot, because you have no faith in me."

He hardly had time to speak another word when confusion broke loose in the synagogue and the townsfolk ended up physically dragging him outside to the edge of the town where they intended to throw him. But wriggling away, he escaped, never—he thought—to return.

Tears welled up in Joshua's eyes as he recalled those sad memories. How different from these simple folk today who hardly knew him, yet trusted him so openly! His own who had grown up with him could find only scorn for him. And he had so much he wanted to share with them.

Joshua turned away and walked toward Cana on his way to Capernaum, though things were vastly changed in the hamlet, even to its name, which was now Kfar Kana. There were hints of sights and places as they once were. The scene of the wedding party rose in his mind with all the fun and dancing and meeting of old friends. Miriam's worries about the wine dissolved with the sudden appearance of a hundred and fifty gallons of excellent vintage. The revelers had already gone through the sixteen-year supply prepared by the bride's father. At Capernaum, Joshua was surprised to find that Peter's house was still standing, not intact, but recognizable. It was the oddest-shaped house in the whole country. Being Peter's could it be anything but unusual? Not far away was the shore where he stood on that early morning after the Resurrection, calling out to the apostles as they fished in vain. There was a little chapel on the spot now, commemorating the event. Joshua stopped at one of the seaside restaurants and bought a roasted fish sandwich and took it with him down along the shore where he sat and ate his supper, dreamily looking out across the sparkling Sea of Galilee, reminiscing over all the memories of times long gone.

As twilight approached he headed up the hillside that rose abruptly from the lake and found a quiet place nestled in a clump of trees overlooking the sea, where he settled down to prayer. Then he lay down, resting his head against the root of a tree, and fell sound asleep.

*   *   *

Sunrise on the Sea of Galilee is spectacular. Vast waters, as far as the eye can see, unlike the oceans, calm, unruffled, sparkling in the orange and yellow brilliance rising from the distant shores. Joshua sat, resting against a tree, soaking in the beauty of the sunrise as it unfolded, thinking that, as breathtaking as it was, it paled in comparison to the beauty of heaven. And yet to his human eye and all his human emotions, the constantly changing colors in the rising sun fascinated him, inspiring a deep sigh. "If people only took time to enjoy the endless beauty my Father has placed in His creation for their enjoyment and contemplation!"

Joshua had many memories of Capernaum, this cosmopolitan community that catered to every describable foreigner passing through for trading or financial purposes. The beautiful synagogue built by a Roman centurion, whose servant Jesus had restored to life, was no longer there, though remains of a later synagogue survived. Its mere presence stimulated memories, the huge crowds who followed him everywhere, from dawn to sunset, their enthusiasm when he first appeared on the scene, and their gradual disillusionment as he showed no interest in assuming power and frowned on accumulating material possessions. Promising them his flesh and blood as the food of their souls was the last straw. He could have sidestepped the crisis, saying it was only symbolic, but he repeated and emphasized even more, "My flesh is real food and my blood is real drink and unless you eat my flesh and drink my blood you have no life in you." What he didn't tell them was how he would do this so it would not be ridiculous. His miracle of the loaves and fishes the day before gave them more than enough reason to believe that if he promised something he could carry it through. But instead they turned their backs on him, shaking their heads and muttering, "This is a hard saying, who can accept it?" as they walked away, never to return.

His discouragement and sense of failure at the time came back to him with a sharpness that revived the same moods all over again. He remembered leaving the area and wandering through the pagan lands up north to calm his troubled soul.

Thinking these things, he left Capernaum and traveled west to Mount Carmel. He was fortunate to be given a ride most of the way, as the Plain of Esdraelon was barren and monotonous, though filled with history as the great battlefield of times past, and the supposed site of the Armageddon, the final battle between good and evil.

Reaching the outskirts of Haifa, Joshua walked up the highway to the top of Mount Carmel, and arrived at the Carmelite monastery a little before supper. A priest by the name of Elias Friedman met him at the entrance. He was a hero in the Jewish resistance in Warsaw and had eventually become a priest and was transferred by his order to Mount Carmel. His greatest dream now was to become an Israeli citizen, which so far had eluded him.

"Shalom," the priest said in greeting.

"Shalom aleichem," Joshua replied, then continued speaking in Hebrew, to the priest's delight. From then on they both spoke in Hebrew. The monk invited Joshua into the church and showed him around, explaining all the details of the history of the place to him. He was surprised to find that Joshua was even more familiar with historical details than he was.

"Many Jewish people have been coming here to our monastery, curious about our history and also curious about Christianity. In fact, we have had so many Jewish people, particularly military, coming here on their day off, that we have had to schedule tours in Hebrew several times a day.

"But, I don't speak to them about Christianity. That is a mixed bag with so many of our people having tragic memories of the cruelty of Christians through the centuries. The churches haven't done justice to Jesus' message either by the way they lived or by the way they complicated his teachings almost beyond recognition.

"What I do is talk to them about Jesus; he was one of ours, you know, and what he was all about and how our people loved him and followed him everywhere, because he spoke directly to their hearts. It made sense to them then, and it makes sense to our people now. People today are no different. They too are looking for what Jesus had to give. But they don't want all the baggage and pettiness of a church with its politics and legalism. They have had their fill of that in their own religion. Jesus' philosophy is something we can handle, something we Jews can be proud of. That's what I talk about and it makes good sense."

Joshua just listened as the high-spirited priest poured out his ideas. "It makes good sense what you say," Joshua told him. "Our people are searching. The old ways no longer have meaning to so many of them. They feel it is tied in with a concept of mission that has passed them by, and does not seem relevant to everyday life in a modern world.

"I have talked to a number of soldiers. I know they don't believe in God, but their lack of faith is not in God as He is, but in God as others have conceived Him and presented Him to them. This god they reject. The fact that they come here shows they are not without faith. They are still searching. You do them a s rvice by presenting to them a Jesus who is reasonable and caring, and a God who is gentle and caring. They need to know they are loved."

Father Elias invited Joshua for supper. Joshua was only too glad to stay. He was introduced to the other priests. Some were friendly; the others gave the impression they couldn't care less. After supper, Elias brought Joshua down to the shrine of Elijah, the founder of their order.

"Some laugh at us for claiming the prophet Elijah as our founder, but he really was. The Bible talks about Elijah founding a school of prophets. They always existed here on

Mount Carmel. When Jesus came, the hermits on Carmel accepted him and always had a special affection for his mother. She may have visited here. When the Crusaders came to the Holy Land, they found the monks living here and admired their way of life. We are still here after surviving all kinds of persecutions. Come, I will drive you down to the shrine of Elijah. It is only a short distance down the road."

As their car exited the parking lot, Joshua noticed the two shadows who had been tailing him across the street from the monastery trying to remain hidden behind a tree.

"That building across the street belongs to the monastery," Elias told Joshua. "Years ago the government took it for a barracks and a radar post. It overlooks the Mediterranean and can scan practically the whole country."

Joshua was impressed with the shrine of Elijah, and the spot where Elijah slew the four hundred priests of Baal and single-handedly, with God's help, brought the whole nation back to the worship of God.

"This shrine is still popular with our people," the priest said. "It is one of the rare authentic sites in our history. Jewish people love to come here, and often bring bus loads of children with them. It is a powerfully inspirational experience."

Joshua stood there looking up at the bigger-than-life statue of Elijah. The statue itself tells a story, and makes an indelible impression.

As the two men were admiring the statue, three reconnaissance jets thundered overhead, shaking the ground beneath them. "Someday, maybe, we will have peace," the priest sighed.

"That will happen only when people decide they want it," Joshua added. "Peace has to be everybody's business."

"I would like to do more for peace, but an individual doesn't even know where to start," Father Elias complained.

"I meet many people who are concerned and want to do

something about it," Joshua told him. "Many of them are Arabs, some are Christian, many are Jews. If you like you can work with us. We are forming a little community."

"Where do you meet?" Elias asked him.

"We are meeting on the Mount of Olives at the Seven Arches Hotel," Joshua told him. "The manager was kind enough to offer us space. You are more than welcome, if you would like to come. Bring a few of your friends, too, if you like."

"I'll be there," the priest promised, then continued his narration about the history of Mount Carmel.

CHAPTER **6**

JOSHUA TRAVELED along the coast, stopping at Caesarea and Tel Aviv, where he picked up more allies, then worked his way back east to Jerusalem. The trip was for the most part uneventful, until he reached Tel Aviv. There he spotted the two agents who had obviously been following him all across the land.

It was in Tel Aviv that Joshua met Bernard Herbstman, a thin, balding rabbi with blue eyes who headed a Reform synagogue—the same rabbi Susan had boasted about a few days before. How they met was bizarre. Joshua had decided to take a walk through a Hasidic neighborhood on a Sabbath afternoon. As if that wasn't bad enough, he was carrying a small backpack with his belongings. Some of the people were offended that he should be so bold as to walk through their quarter in violation of the Sabbath. Not having any of the trappings of a Hasid, it seemed only too obvious that he was intentionally challenging their laws and their beliefs. Perhaps he was. Joshua had always been bothered by the nonsensical rules concocted in the name of religion, which stripped the joy out of life and turned God's children into caricatures. Besides, it gave God a bad name, which to Joshua was really offensive.

Whatever his motive, the residents took offense and confronted him. The discussion became heated, more so since Joshua was so cool and unperturbable.

"You know our laws and our customs. Why do you violate them and insult us by invading our neighborhood?" one man said heatedly.

"I do not come to insult anyone. I come to visit a friend," Joshua retorted.

"One of us?" the man said, shocked. "Where does he live?"

"On the other side of the neighborhood," Joshua answered.

"Why didn't you walk around the neighborhood, so we wouldn't have to see you?" the man asked indignantly.

"Because it doesn't make sense. It's almost a mile longer," Joshua answered.

Trying to prevent Joshua from continuing, the two men stood in front of him, and soon others came to their aid, refusing Joshua passage through their neighborhood.

"You people think you are honoring God by acting like this," Joshua said pointedly. "Instead, you make of God a fool like yourselves, living a way God never commanded, paralyzing people's minds, and forcing people to live in fear and bondage."

At that point Rabbi Herbstman, who saw the confrontation from his car window as he drove down past the entrance to the neighborhood, stopped and approached the group and tried to mediate. They insulted him, saying he wasn't even a Jew, since he belonged to a Reform synagogue.

"Mister," the rabbi said to Joshua, "come with me. I have a car. I will drive you where you want to go. Come with me, these people are unreasonable. You can't talk to them. They'll end up stoning you. I know them. They live in another world."

Realizing that he was getting nowhere, Joshua left with Rabbi Herbstman. He drove him where he was headed, and in fact he knew the people. They were Hasidim, but they were good friends. The family was also friends of Aaron Bessmer, who had insisted Joshua visit them when he came to Tel Aviv.

When they opened the door and saw the rabbi, they welcomed him with open arms. He then introduced Joshua to them, and they all retired to the yard for refreshments.

"Aaron told us about you, Joshua," said Moshe, the man of the house and Aaron's good friend. Moshe was a rotund and jolly fellow. "And we had sort of a premonition of your coming. We just got a phone call from a friend at the other end of the neighborhood, telling us about a stranger creating a scuffle over there. My wife made the remark, 'I wonder if that's Aaron's friend, who's supposed to come to visit us. It sounds like him.' And sure enough, here you are."

Everyone laughed.

"Rabbi, it is a real honor having you visit us. We don't see you that often," Moshe's wife, Rose, said.

"Thank you," the rabbi answered. "But you have to admit, you almost have to have a visa to get in here. Fortunately, I know the back way and have a car. Today I was on an errand of mercy, otherwise I wouldn't have been driving over this way."

"I hope you can stay awhile. Lou and Toby are coming with friends of theirs, Forrest and Katherine. They said Forrest is Jewish somewhere in his background, but I think she's joking. Tom said he's a brilliant man, supposed to have fed half the Jewish population of New York with his kosher chickens years ago. Toby and Lou would love to see you, Rabbi—you have to stay," Moshe said to his friend. "In fact, we have a nice spread prepared for them, ready since yesterday, of course."

"Of course," the rabbi said with a knowing smile.

"Joshua," Moshe said, "you have a reputation for being quite a mystery man. Tell us, what brings you up this way?"

"I guess I've been on assignment. I'm sure Aaron has

briefed you on what we are doing," Joshua replied.

"Yes, he's all fired up about it, thanks to you. He's even got us committed to coming to Jerusalem for the meeting next week. Bernie will have to come, too. This will be right up your alley, Bernie," Moshe said to his friend.

"What's it all about, if you don't mind my asking before you sign me up?" the rabbi said.

"Not at all," Rose said. "Aaron's been involved with a group of people trying to promote peace. They haven't had much luck except with other Jews. They've been trying in vain for years to interest leading Arabs, but without success. Then, along comes Joshua and snags a sheik and all his family to join forces. We are having a meeting in Jerusalem this coming Wednesday night. It could be the beginning of great things, especially with Joshua here involved."

"Sounds like it might work. At least it has potential with the kinds of people involved," the rabbi said. "They certainly aren't just a group of do-gooders. Yes, you can count me in. I'll bring some of my people with me. There are some government officials in my congregation I can count on."

Lou and Toby and their friends Forrest and Katherine finally arrived. They were charming people, though not the type to become involved in peace movements. As they all settled down to the festivities, Joshua became the center of attention, as if they had known him all their lives.

"We have a priest friend in the States who is very interested in Joshua," Lou said, then looking at Joshua, continued, "He would like your kind of message. We will have to tell him all about you when we go back."

"I'd like to meet him someday," Joshua responded.

"Joshua, where are you off to from here?" Rabbi Herbstman asked.

"Jerusalem."

"I'm driving to Jerusalem tomorrow, so if you don't mind

staying over at my house, you can ride with me if you like," the rabbi said.

"That's better than walking," Joshua responded. "I appreciate your hospitality."

Later in the evening when the party broke up, Moshe promised to come to the meeting on the next Wednesday. Joshua bid his friends shalom, and he and the rabbi left together.

"They are fine people," the rabbi said to Joshua, "so different from most of the people who live there. I'm surprised they stay. They don't have too many friends in their neighborhood."

"I can understand that," Joshua replied. "Yes, they are exceptional people and have caught the genuine religious spirit. God intended the Sabbath to be a day of joy and recreation and a time to visit with family and friends. Religious people have turned that beautiful gift of God into a nightmare, booby-trapped with endless restrictions. These people understand its real meaning and truly enjoy it. Visiting them was fun."

The next day Bernie and Joshua drove from Tel Aviv to Jerusalem. It was less than an hour's ride, but in that time the two men became fast friends as they shared many ideas about God, about religion, about peace. When they arrived in the city, Bernie was surprised when Joshua asked to be dropped off at Ben-Yehuda Street. He expected to drop him off at his residence. When Joshua told him he had none, Bernie said, "You mean you are homeless!"

"I suppose if you want to say that, but it is by choice," Joshua replied.

"You're a mystery, Joshua," Bernie said in bewilderment.

The rabbi left Joshua, promising to be at the meeting. Joshua wandered the neighborhood until his friends gathered later on. He obviously had much to tell them, giving them the names and addresses and phone numbers of everyone who had committed themselves. Their staff would contact each one and provide them with all necessary details. Aaron again surprised Joshua with his efficiency by informing him that he knew of his latest confrontation with the Hasidic group in Tel Aviv.

Joshua merely laughed. "You amaze me, Aaron. It happened only yesterday afternoon. I thought you were supposed to be relaxing on the Sabbath and not doing any work."

"We never relax, you know that," Aaron quipped. "We also found out that your two friends have been following you every place you went."

"I know. I saw them in Haifa on Mount Carmel," Joshua told him.

"By the way, you are not too bad yourself," Susan remarked. "You rattled off all those names and addresses and phone numbers without even referring to a note."

Joshua smiled. "Some things you don't forget," he commented.

"We will contact all these people, then hope they all show up next week," Susan said. Then they all sat back and relaxed while they enjoyed their refreshments. "Joshua," Susan said quietly, "why don't you say a prayer with me over the food and ask God to bless me?" A little embarrassed at being singled out, he agreed and said a beautiful prayer. "Father, we thank you for one another and our friendship. Bless this delightful food which you have given for our pleasure. Bless the work to which we have committed ourselves. May our efforts bring peace to our people and draw them closer to you. And Father be always by our side and in our hearts." The others answered, "Amen." Then they enjoyed each other's friendship, sharing notes over all that had transpired since they were together last.

CHAPTER 7

ARON, SUSAN, and Joshua were the first to arrive for the meeting at the Seven Arches. The evening was blessedly cool, a night when people wouldn't mind going out. Long before the scheduled time, people of all kinds began filing into the hotel. All Joshua's newfound friends came, every one of them, Arabs, Jews, Christians, priests, imams, Rabbi Herbstman. In time the spacious room was filled. The last to arrive was the sheik, Ibrahim Saud, with a retinue of important family members from all across the land. Joshua met him at the door and the two men embraced and kissed each other on both cheeks. Aaron and his friends were amazed. When Sheik Ibrahim entered the room, everyone stood and began to applaud. The sheik was taken aback by all the attention but composed himself and responded with a pleasant smile of appreciation, then took his seat with everyone else.

The meeting was called to order by Daniel Sharon. Daniel Sharon's family were old Jewish pioneers who had settled in Palestine early in the century, early settlers who had befriended their Arab neighbors and developed many solid friendships among many local Arab residents. In fact, Daniel's sister was married to an Arab, a pious man who attended Jewish services as well as services at the mosque. Daniel, together with a number of others, had been trying to foster better relationships among all the peoples in their communities. Their greatest opposition, however, came from militantly religious people who felt he was undermining their culture and their religious ideals by fostering the integration of people with different religions. Daniel began by introducing himself and the others in the core group, last of all Joshua.

"I must tell you, my friends, I owe my life to this man," Daniel said. "Last week Joshua was a total stranger to me. I met him for the first time on the street and he warned me not to take my car home. I went back into my office at the government building and had my car checked. It had been booby-trapped. I don't know how he knew about it. I don't even know how he knew me. He himself was a stranger here in town until the very moment we met on the street. But I shall be forever grateful to him for saving my life.

"I would like now to turn the meeting over to Colonel Aaron Bessmer, who has dedicated so much of his time and talent to bring peace to our land. Aaron is a highly respected military officer on the general staff, and is totally dedicated to peace. Colonel Bessmer."

"Thank you, Dan. I am glad you are still with us. I must admit I am overwhelmed by the number of people and the composition of the group here this evening. The story Dan just told you is true, and I must admit, as a military officer, I was a bit skeptical about Joshua when I heard about the incident of Dan's car, and wondered just how Joshua knew about the bomb. But over the past couple of weeks I have learned not to be surprised about anything that this man might know or do. The success of tonight's meeting is due largely to him, who has no car, no telephone, not even a home or a bed to sleep in, yet he traveled the length and breadth of this land touching people's hearts and, like a magnet, drawing them to this meeting.

"I know the many things I would like to say to you all. But, being who I am and what I am, my words might not be understood in the way I mean them. Since so many of you

are here tonight because of Joshua, I would like to introduce him and let him speak to you. He has captured in his
person the dream we all aspire to.

"Joshua, would you please step up here and speak to this
wonderful group of people?"

Everyone applauded as Joshua approached the microphone. Aaron shook his hand warmly and then sat down.

"My friends, your presence here this evening is impres-
sive. We are Jews, and Arabs, Christians of all sorts, men
and women, and even some children. I am grateful to all of
you for coming. It took a bold leap of faith and trust in the
future to come here. It was not an easy decision, and one
for which many will demand an explanation, an explanation
that cannot be easily given, and even less easily understood.
I admire you for your courage and for your love and concern for your children's future. That is really what is at
stake here: the kind of life we are willing to bequeath to
our children.

"Aaron mentioned I have nothing. That is true. I need
little, a little food perhaps, and water, a few clothes people
give me, and my Father in heaven takes care of the rest. I
walk without fear. I am not odd, and I am not a freak. I just
enjoy being free. I care about my people, and you are all
my people because you are all the beloved children of God,
and we all belong to one another. I feel just as much a part
of Sheik Ibrahim's family as I do a part of Aaron's family.
God is not Arab or Jew or Christian. He is the Father of all.
He has bestowed different gifts and different lights upon all
of you, not to make you proud and elite and alien to one
another, but that you might share with one another those
special gifts.

"We live in a troubled land. We are all Semites. We are
all the children of common ancestors. We are closer to one
another than most other tribes and races on this earth. Yet
we live in fear and distrust of one another. It is not right. It
is not healthy. And it is all so unnecessary.

"We are all here tonight because we realize that, and at great personal risk we have decided to do something about it. Before all else it is important for us to realize that God is not pleased with hatred and distrust, and He abominates terrorism, which destroys the living temples of His presence in the world. No excuse can shield those perpetrators from the awful judgment of God.

"And we all must remember, there is only one God. There is not a god of the Christian, and a god of the Jew, and a god of the Muslim. There is one God, who is Lord and Father of us all. He looks upon all of us as His children, and we must have enough faith to see each other through God's eyes, and to show understanding and concern for one another.

"It is not easy to reverse the trend of fear and suspicion that has been our heritage, but that trend must be reversed. We can start here. It will take time, and discipline. We can teach our children to love and care for one another. Religion should not be a divisive force, as it has been for so many centuries. True religion is the living expression of God's wisdom and love, and a truly religious person will reflect that wisdom and love of God to all he or she touches and will be a powerful source of peace and goodness to everyone. No one need fear a truly religious person, because he carries in his heart the living presence of God, and blesses everyone he meets.

"So our movement starting here tonight has to start with God. He is the only bond who can unite us. This should be our first lesson, to find again our Heavenly Father, and allow Him to come into our hearts, so we can begin this noble journey toward peace. The people who manage this beautiful hotel have graciously offered us their facilities for our meetings. We will meet again next week. I hope you will all feel comfortable enough to bring your families. May you all have a safe journey home."

Joshua received a standing ovation which lasted for a full

five minutes before Aaron could begin his closing remarks and dismiss the group.

Sheik Ibrahim approached Joshua after the meeting and thanked him for touching his life so deeply. The sheik assured him his whole family would be solidly behind him. He then asked Joshua if he would mind if he looked upon him as his family's imam, to which Joshua said he would be honored.

Other people Joshua had called during the recent weeks came up to him and told him how impressed they were with what he had to say. They said he seemed transformed as he spoke and seemed to radiate the wisdom of God Himself. And to think they had looked upon him as just a simple wanderer when they had first met him. Many left with tears in their eyes and a new feeling of hope in their hearts.

The old Franciscan priest was there with a good number of his friends, including an Orthodox priest. Next to him sat the monk from Mount Carmel and also Rabbi Herbstman, who was deeply touched by what Joshua said. These all came over to Joshua after the crowd had thinned out and expressed their thanks and admiration. The old priest said that when he closed his eyes during the talk, he thought he was hearing Jesus speak.

Daniel Sharon made a warm gesture of gratitude to Sheik Ibrahim for coming to the meeting. The sheik told him it was out of loyalty to his friend, Joshua, that he came. He then told Daniel that he too was blessed by Joshua's goodness and related the story of his granddaughter, the lamb, and the miraculous curing of the snakebite. Both men went home wondering about this man who could touch people's hearts and even their lives so intimately.

After the meeting broke up, Aaron, Dan, Joshua, and their original group went over to Ben-Yehuda Street for refreshments and debriefing. Aaron leaned back contentedly and observed, "What we saw tonight is the beginning of a wholly new community composed of Arabs, Jews, and Christians."

Joshua just listened, thoughtfully weighing everything, happy at the blessed changes in so many hearts.

8

THE NEXT DAY Joshua walked through Jerusalem. The old section was so much as he had remembered it with all the smells and sights and haggling over prices in the markets along the streets and back alleys. As he walked along, he was again conscious of being followed. Walking around the corner and up a side street, he looked back and saw two men among the pedestrians walking up the street, the same men he had seen everyplace else. He also noticed, following in the distance behind the two men, a boy. He had seen the boy on one other occasion at the sheik's camp. Now he was certain the young fellow was following the two men, though so far in the distance they would never have suspected it. He recognized the boy as one of the sheik's grandsons and wondered what he was doing in Jerusalem.

Joshua knew the two shadows had nowhere near his stamina, so he decided to give them a good day's exercise. The next few hours he wandered all through the city, going up to the Temple Mount and visiting the smaller El-Aqsa mosque. There he stayed, praying for almost an hour while the two men stood out in the blazing sun, each ruing the day he took the job. The young boy positioned himself in the crowd at the other end of the square, waiting, watching.

The day finally ended uneventfully. When Joshua left the mosque, he continued his walk through the city, then worked his way over to Bethany, where like old times, he spent the night.

The two men disappeared. The boy went home and reported to his father what had transpired during the day.

The next day over lunch, Susan remarked to Aaron and a few of their friends how well the meeting had gone the night before. "Do you realize," she said, "that all those people Joshua got to come were total strangers to him just a week ago? How did he know he could trust them? How did they know they could trust him? How did he know where to find them? They are from all over the country. He couldn't have done any better if he had the intelligence service working with him. And for some strange reason, they are already completely dedicated to him."

"I noticed that myself," Samuel remarked. "The sheik looks at him with almost veneration. I think he would do anything for him."

At that point Daniel Sharon came into the cafeteria and sat down with the others.

"Continuing last night's debriefing?" he said.

"Just about," Aaron answered. "We were remarking how uncanny it was that Joshua could so easily have picked all those people to come to last night's meeting in so short a time, and he never even knew them before."

"Well, I found out why the sheik is so committed," Daniel said, with an evident note of triumph in his voice.

"Why is that?" Susan asked.

"Joshua saved his granddaughter's life," Daniel replied.

"How so?" Samuel questioned.

"Well," Daniel continued, "the sheik and I talked after the meeting last night and compared notes. I told him about the car incident, and he told me about Joshua visiting their camp at the oasis. During the night a viper bit his granddaughter, and the whole family was beside themselves, unable to get the girl to a hospital at that time of the night. Well, it seems Joshua ended up curing the girl. Even the bite marks disappeared. Needless to say, the whole family was overwhelmed. The sheik is convinced that Joshua is a prophet of some kind and he and his family are totally committed to following him. He even asked Joshua if he would be his family's imam. Imagine that, and they all know Joshua is a Jew."

"How did he cure her?" Susan asked.

"It seems he just touched her and told her to be well and she recovered immediately," Daniel replied. "The sheik attributes it to his being so close to Allah. And if the sheik and his family feel this way about him, who knows what all the others experienced when they met him? After what happened to me last week I would believe anything he told me."

"Yet he seems so normal and so down-to-earth," Aaron remarked. "He doesn't seem especially pious or religious. He's just ordinary, like us."

"I guess that's what's so beautiful about him," Susan added. "You feel you've known him all your life."

"Well, he's got the Mossad standing on their heads," Aaron interjected. "They don't know what to make of him. Gus, my friend over there, told me they are baffled by his continually meeting with Arabs of all sorts, and they all know he is a Jew. They are convinced he is up to something, but they can't put their fingers on it. He seems innocent enough on the surface. His objectives remain a mystery. They have him on continuous surveillance, but he eludes them."

"I think he is just a good man with few needs who has found peace within himself and wants to help others find peace. I think it is as simple as that," Samuel added. "I think he is a rare, innocent individual who is authentically holy and has nothing of the self-righteous about him. If that's subversive, then our world is no longer fit for good people to live in."

"Susan thinks he's special, too," Aaron said flippantly.

"Aaron, you're being wise," Susan shot back at him. "I think he's a very unusual person, but a bit too unworldly for me. I admit I do have a deep admiration for him."

"We all do," Aaron added as everyone finished lunch and started back to work.

That same afternoon Joshua was taken by some of his Arab friends to visit the sheik, who had requested a meeting with him. His family had moved to a site closer to the villages where grazing was better.

"Salaam, my saintly friend," the sheik said as he welcomed Joshua and kissed him with all due ceremony.

"Salaam, my dear friend," Joshua said returning the greeting. The family were all excited at seeing Joshua again, the children especially, who ran over to him and grabbed his hands and his clothes. Joshua spoke with them briefly until the sheik ushered him into his tent where they could talk privately.

After small talk while they partook of light refreshments, the sheik came to the point of their meeting.

"Joshua," he began, "I must tell you I came away from your meeting the other night deeply moved. It is only recently, now that I am an old man, that I have begun to think along the lines on which you spoke. You touched me by your ability to rise above pettiness and hurt and find goodness in people who might have been your enemies. That is a new thinking for me, and I find it hard to comprehend. Could you explain to me why you can feel that way?"

"Ibrahim," Joshua answered, "you are a good man, and you are trying sincerely to find the kingdom of God. But you look in the wrong direction. God's thoughts are not our thoughts. We look at people and measure their worth and their goodness in their relationship to ourselves. God as a loving Father sees the intrinsic goodness in each of His children. People are not evil. They are easily hurt and they hurt back, because of pride and because of fear. It is to protect themselves. It is not because they are evil. Some have been so deeply hurt and damaged they strike back at everyone indiscriminately. They become deranged.

"A person who is close to God learns to see others through God's eyes. As your prophet writes so frequently, 'Allah is all compassionate.' He sees the hurt and the anguish, and the reasons why people do hurtful things. God tries always to heal. The closer a person comes to God, the more that person reflects His healing love. Anger and vengeance have no place in a soul where God dwells, only forgiveness and understanding.

"You ask why I can feel this way. Since my beginning, God possessed me. I have always been a clear vessel of His love for His children. When people do hurtful things, I see their hurt and I seek only to soothe their hurt and heal their wounds. Since my life is in my Father's hands I cannot be threatened, so I fear no one. They cannot hurt me, so I feel no need to strike out and destroy. It is a goal all God's children should strive for. It is the key to peace."

"Joshua, I think that is the reason I love you," the old man said. "You are so pure. Evil has never touched your soul. Only God can feel the way you feel and, as much as I respect you, I do not think I can rise to those heights of holiness.

"I used to hate, when I was younger. It is hard to see our people who lived here for over a thousand years be driven into camps behind barbed wire and treated like animals. But I know that hatred is not good for the soul, so I have risen above the hatred that once possessed me. However, I still cannot forgive, and to love is impossible. Yet I see the damage my past hatred has caused in my family. My son is consumed with hatred. I am afraid. I spend many nights without sleep fearing the future.

"I know that forgiveness is the only way to peace. My people are unable to forgive. The Jews are unable to forgive. What do we do, kill each other until no one is left?

"Your way, Joshua, is the only way to peace. That is why I admire what you are doing. You are the only one who has been able to gather our people and the Jews and the Christians together to talk to one another.

"I am an old man, Joshua, and it is hard for me to change, but I want to do what is good for my children and my people. I assure you of my own and my family's support for what you are doing."

"Ibrahim, you are not far from the path of godliness. In time you will reach what you are striving for," Joshua assured him. "We cannot change overnight what has taken a lifetime to cultivate. In time we will rise above the pettiness of being human and reach across the chasm of ignorance and hatred to embrace those who are fearful and hostile. When that happens, the children will reap the harvest."

When the two men finished talking, Joshua left and was driven back to the city. The sheik did not tell Joshua that he was being followed by the two intelligence people and that he had instructed his grandson to follow the two men and report back to him anything that should happen. Joshua already knew it.

Joshua also knew that the sheik's son Khalil was plotting with Arab radicals to ambush and assassinate him for trying to bring about peace. Joshua knew the old man sensed something, and it was breaking his heart knowing his son was up to something evil. The sheik was also overwhelmed with guilt that he had instilled the hatred in his son that was now bearing such bitter fruit. That is the paradox of hatred, that it destroys the children of those who nourish it, a poisoned heritage to one's own offspring.

9

THE NEXT meeting of
Aaron and Joshua's group, the Children of Peace, took place
as scheduled, at the Seven Arches Hotel. This time, however, the crowd was so large the hotel was unable to accommodate it, so the meeting had to be held outdoors. The
manager was more than gracious in offering the assistance
of his staff to facilitate all the changes necessary, like moving
the speaker system outdoors and rearranging all the chairs.
Not only did the other members of the sheik's extended
family come to the meeting, but relatives and friends of
people Joshua had invited to the first meeting. Rabbi
Herbstman brought a sizable number from his congregation. A large contingent of Arab Christians came all the way
from Ramallah, a city with an Arab Christian population of
over fifty thousand, and many others from Nazareth. They
had all come to hear the speaker who had held the people at
the last meeting spellbound. His reputation had spread far
and wide.

He did not disappoint them. After the usual introductory
comments and recognizing of important personages in
attendance, Aaron turned the meeting over to Susan, who
introduced Joshua to the newcomers. Resting his folded
hands on the lectern, he began:

"My friends, it is not by chance or by circumstance that
you are here this evening. The spirit of God has touched

each of you. You are special and have been called. You all
have realized, each in your own way, and by your own experiences, that peace in our land is long past due. If there is
to be peace, it must come from the people. Leaders forever
find reasons to postpone peace and at times to upset the
peace. Peace is not always in their best interest. If people
want peace, they must seize the peace.

"But it will not come without hard work.

"We are all children of a common Father, a Father who
loves you with a love beyond understanding, a love that is
so tender that He watches over you day and night, not with
a critical eye, but with a mother's love, protecting you each
day from a thousand dangers. Even though tragedy sometimes strikes, through sickness or human cruelty, your
Father is always nearby to heal your wounds and offer His
love if only you open your hearts to Him."

As Joshua was speaking, he could see diverse groups
spread throughout the audience. He spotted Khalil's terrorist friends and also the two detectives who were tailing him
day and night. Sitting together was a group of Hasidim,
curious as to what this man was teaching, whether it would
strengthen their oneness as a people or threaten the purity
of their goals. They listened intently. Joshua's memory
soared back through history and saw Pharisees all over
again, Pharisees in modern, well, not-so-modern dress. He
wondered if he could reach them or if they were like their
ancient counterparts, frozen in their thoughts, like automa-
tons in lock step, unable to think in any way other than the
way their leader told them they could think. Joshua sensed
their minds were already closed. He could see opposing
forces already beginning to take shape, as they had once,
long ago. This time, though, he knew things were different.

"We live in difficult yet exciting times, times in which
each individual can make his or her mark on history. We
cannot face the future with fear, we must face it boldly. We
cannot look to a future with total isolation from the world

around us. We live in a world fashioned by God in such a way that we all need one another as members of a family. Isolation is a refusal to love, a rejection of others around you. It calls forth the bitterest feelings of resentment and recrimination, because it is a self-righteous rejection of your neighbor whom God said you should love. Isolation is foreign to God, who wants His children to love and help one another and build up a community of shared concern and mutual enrichment. Religion that regards as evil contact with others whom God created is not a religion that has come from God. It creates an infection in the community. It causes its members to withdraw their love from the community around them. It creates a vacuum that becomes filled with resentment and alienation and draws upon itself recriminations and hostility.

"If there is to be peace, it must begin in the hearts of each one of us. It must become a way of life, a seed that grows like a beautiful flower spreading its fragrance throughout the whole garden.

"Peace cannot grow where there are angry and hostile thoughts. Peace must come from a mind that is pure and gentle and free from meanness and suspicion.

"Peace can flow only from a soul that sees the goodness in others and is willing to excuse and repair their faults.

"Peace must be loving parents' first gift to their children, the soil in which the most beautiful gifts of grace can then flourish.

"Peace flows from the heart of God and like a soothing balm bathes the soul it touches in its delicate perfume.

"If you want peace, open your hearts to let God enter. Do not be afraid of Him. He wants nothing from you. He wants only to give you His love and His peace and His freedom. When you leave here this evening, do not go alone. Walk home with God in your heart, and bring Him home to your families. Teach your children to open their hearts to Him, so they can find Him early in their lives and not make the mistake so many make in looking for Him when their lives are almost over."

All during Joshua's talk the audience sat spellbound. No one had ever heard anyone speak like this before. Each heart was filled with a peace and a lightness it had never experienced. The audience was reluctant to leave and wished Joshua would continue speaking.

When the talk ended, Aaron got up and after a few business items suggested that, since there were so many people from Galilee, it was only fair they have their next meeting in Galilee. Joshua suggested the hillside outside Capernaum overlooking the Sea of Galilee as the site. They set the date and decided it should be in the afternoon. The people were to bring their own lunch. The meeting broke up with everyone hugging each other. Some Jews and Arabs had never hugged each other before. It brought many tears of joy and forgiveness, and a sense of wonder at how simple it could be.

The next day Joshua went to the Temple Mount and prayed in the Mosque of Omar. Many of his friends were there worshiping. Afterward they gathered outside and spoke freely with him. Some of their neighbors joined in, anxious to meet the man they had heard so much about. It was a new experience for the Temple Mount to witness Arabs and a Jew talking in so friendly a manner, and openly.

As the group broke up, Joshua sat down and looked across the square, reminiscing. This had once been the sight of the glorious temple built by Herod, with its beautiful golden roof and frieze work, and rich marble and other stones rare to the area, and delicately designed porticoes surrounding the vast courtyard. Here, long ago, the Son of God spoke often. Here, Jewish people by the hundreds would gather to listen to him, and be mesmerized by His teaching and touched by his healing of the troubled and the crippled. The priests and politicians were furious at his boldness in daring to meet with the people right at the very seat of their power. He called them "whitewashed sepulchers so nice to look at on the outside, but on the inside full of filth and dead men's bones," and excoriated them for stripping the joy out of people's relationships with their heavenly Father and for "laying heavy burdens on people's shoulders and not lifting a finger to lighten those burdens." Hypocrites he called them. They were stung to fury at his audacity and beside themselves because the common people loved him.

And here it was that one day a group of Pharisees dragged a woman found in adultery through the crowd and flung her at the Teacher's feet, demanding he tell them whether they should follow Moses' command to stone such a one to death or ignore Moses' law and let her go. Disgusted he turned his back and ignored them. When they persisted, he turned and said, "If that is the law, then stone her to death, but let him who is without sin among you cast the first stone." When they picked up stones to kill her, he knelt down and began to write in the dust, looking up at each one, "Oh, yes, I know all about you," and then proceeded to write their secret sins in the dirt. When they saw what he was doing they dropped their stones and slinked away.

Standing up, he said to the woman shivering at his feet, "Is there no one to condemn you, woman?"

"No one, Lord."

"Neither will I condemn you. Go and sin no more."

Joshua sat there wrapped in memory. It seemed like just yesterday. And he wondered how the Pharisees were able to find someone committing adultery, and only the woman at that. It will always be an enigma how merciful is God and how unforgiving sinners are toward other sinners.

Sitting there, watching people walking back and forth, mostly Arabs and small groups of tourists, Joshua wondered why his group couldn't also worship together at this site. But then he realized that what is important to his Father is not the place where people worship but what is in their hearts. With that thought Joshua rose and left the site, wandering through the streets of the old city, talking to people, comforting the sick and the elderly as he passed by their ancient hovels. He was becoming a common sight in the neighborhood, and people found themselves looking forward to his passing through. There were even rumors of desperately ill people being cured as he passed by and touched them.

Every street had a hundred memories. This was his beloved city. Arriving at an intersection, he noticed a sign on a stone wall, VIA DOLOROSA, the Way of Sorrows. Looking one way down the narrow street he recognized the approach to the Roman soldiers' quarters. Here the Son of God was held prisoner during his trial and here he was beaten by the soldiers. In the opposite direction, the street ascended slowly. Along the street were stations, the stops on the way to Calvary venerated by pious disciples through the centuries.

Joshua stopped at the spot where he met his mother, who had been waiting for him as he stumbled along on his death march. She had been used to pain and suffering ever since the priest Simeon prophesied that her son "was destined for the rise and fall of many in Israel and her own soul a sword would pierce." But the pain he saw on his mother's face that day was almost too much for him to bear. She, of all his disciples and loved ones, was the one pure innocent soul who was totally possessed by God since her very beginning and had never harmed a creature. To see her in such pain and torment was indeed a keen agony. His one comfort was that he would appear to her in three days and her joy then would be endless, and the pain would be no more. Tears welled up in Joshua's eyes. He walked on, and then out of

JOSHUA IN THE HOLY LAND   83

the city, around to Siloam, where he visited his friends farming on the banks of the brook.

They had been at the meetings and were impressed with this simple man. Now they felt honored that he would come to visit them in their fields while they were working. They offered him a cup of water from the brook. It was cool, fresh water. The last time Joshua passed through he was a stranger. Now he was a friend and they treated him as such. They wanted him to stay with them, but he was on his way to visit some of the people farther down the valley. They knew he was going there to visit the poor. They gave him a sackful of vegetables from the field to bring to them. Then he filled his canteen in the stream and continued on his way.

He had made the remark two thousand years before, "The poor you will always have with you," and here he was visiting them in their hovels centuries later. They didn't care that he was Jewish. They saw only a man full of love and genuine concern, and they opened their hearts to him. He had nothing of value to give them in any material way, but what he gave them was a sense that a saintly presence was touching their lives and they felt not only honored, but touched by the grace of God's presence. Joshua stopped at the home of the poorest and gave them the bagful of food. They were grateful and insisted he stay and have something to eat with them, which he did. They had others staying with them, neighbors whose simple homes were bulldozed a few days before. Joshua spent some of the time sitting in an open yard talking to the children, telling them stories and playing tricks for them.

The father of the family was named Mohammed. His wife's name was Iffat. They had five children, aged four to sixteen. At the supper table, Mohammed poured his heart out to Joshua, telling him of the cruelty of the military and the harsh way they treated the people. The homes of their neighbors who were staying with them were mistakenly destroyed in retaliation for an ambush in which two soldiers had been killed. But it was others who were responsible for the ambush. These people were innocent.

Joshua listened. It was the same complaint his people had had long ago when the Romans occupied their land. They treated the Jews the same way.

"The problems will resolve themselves in time," Joshua said. "For now, bear with it for your children's sake. They will be the only ones to reap a harvest of bitterness. We must all work together with others of goodwill and put endless pressure on political leaders to give justice to your people. It must be done peacefully."

"It is easy to talk like that," Mohammed complained to Joshua, "but when you have to live this way day after day, it is demeaning and makes one ashamed in front of his own family."

"Anger and vengeance is no solution," Joshua said calmly. "It hardens everyone and turns even the good and well-intentioned against your cause. With your neighbors and friends you must continually present your cause. As your numbers grow, the pressure mounts, and good people will see the justice of your cause and mount their own pressure. In time it will have its effect. Even now you can see that good people are willing to work for peace, even among the soldiers. So you must have patience but constantly work for peace and justice."

"When people are hurting, it is hard to have patience," Iffat said.

"I know," Joshua answered, "but discipline tempers the frustration and cools the burning coals. It is the only way."

When the supper ended, Joshua asked Allah's blessing on the family and left, walking down through the village speaking to the people as they sat in front of their houses, playing cards or solving the world's problems.

As night began to fall, Joshua walked up into the hills

and, resting under a spreading olive tree, shared the day's experiences with his Father, then fell into a deep sleep.

The next day Joshua spent wandering through the area sightseeing and talking to people he met along the way. Every place he went he noticed the same two men following him, and the Arab boy in the distance. Or rather, boys, for now there were two Arab boys; it seemed they were taking turns.

That night Joshua met his friends Aaron and Susan and the others on Ben-Yehuda Street. They had their usual dessert and coffee and talked about the vast progress made within the past few weeks, and how everyone was looking forward to the "picnic" up in Galilee. They were happy to share with Joshua that a good number of their friends in the army would be coming with them, impressed with what had been happening the past few weeks. They wanted very much to be part of it.

"You don't know what a breakthrough that is, Joshua," Susan commented. "These are people who have been hard-nosed over peace issues, and used to laugh at Aaron and myself when we talked about such things. I suppose we shouldn't be surprised, even my parents don't really approve of what I am doing. By the way, Joshua, my parents would love to meet you. Do you think you might come over to our house, sometime?"

"Yes, whenever you like," Joshua answered.

"You sure it's your parents, Susan?" Aaron quipped with a broad grin.

"Don't be wise, Aaron," Susan shot back. "I'd love to have him, too, but it was my parents who asked."

"Joshua, how do you keep so calm and so relaxed with the uptight people you mingle with all day long?" Samuel asked. "I watch you and you don't seem to have a nerve in your body."

"Oh, I guess it's just that I know people and what is in their hearts, and they know I care and they trust me, so I can feel comfortable working with them," Joshua answered simply.

"I'm amazed," Samuel said, as he sipped his cappuccino.

"Joshua," Aaron said, "I don't know how you intended to get up to Galilee, but if you like you are more than welcome to ride with me. My family and I will be going up the day before."

"That's very thoughtful of you. I appreciate it. It would be a long walk," Joshua responded.

The group broke up before long. As they were leaving, Susan arranged to pick up Joshua the next evening and bring him to her house for supper, so her parents could meet him.

The next day went fast, and toward evening Susan promptly met Joshua and took him to her home. She wasn't dressed like a soldier this time. Her outfit was simple yet tasteful, and her hair had been done that very day. Susan's parents were dignified people in their early sixties. They had seen much heartache and misery in their lifetimes, and it had scarred them but not embittered them. Her father's name was Moshe. He was a tall man, with a full head of white hair, steel blue eyes, and a slightly aquiline nose. He had the elegant grace of a man who might be a diplomat. He was affable and had a keen sense of humor.

Susan's mother was dressed like the cook she was that evening. When Joshua arrived, she was in the kitchen cooking, perspiring over the hot stove. She gave the impression of being a strong woman who had had to make many hard decisions in her life and was quite capable of handling any difficult situations that might present themselves. As she held out her hand to greet Joshua, he could tell by her strong grip that here was a woman like the ones written about in the Bible, a strong woman well capable of managing her affairs.

They soon sat down and relaxed, and after simple refreshments, had their supper. Susan's parents knew their daughter was very taken with Joshua, and they were curious to know all about him, where he was from, what he worked at, what was his goal in life. Joshua smiled at the simplicity of their questioning and answered them as well as he could. What could he say? His origins were incomprehensible, he had no family, he had no job. He went about talking to people. It seemed to add up to nothing that any mother would want to see her daughter involved in.

The fact that he was changing the whole face of the nation by doing nothing of apparent significance would never show on a resume, because all he did was talk to people. The fact that he was Susan's hero could not be translated into anything of any substance. But he was likable enough, and so they decided to enjoy the evening and let the future take care of itself.

It turned out to be a pleasant evening. Before the evening was out, both Susan's mother and father were totally enamored of this lovable dreamer. He had to stay for the evening. There was no way they were going to send him out to sleep under some tree somewhere. So he stayed for the night. He and Susan stayed up late, sitting in the garden enjoying the coolness of the night and sharing dreams. Susan knew Joshua liked her and was thrilled he would share his thoughts and dreams with her. She in turn poured her heart out to him, at one point resting her hand on his as she explained all she had been trying to accomplish with her peace project and how nothing had come of it until Joshua appeared that day on the Mount of Olives. Her whole life's dream began to come to life, and it was so beautiful that he was part of it. They sat talking until late, then Susan showed him to his room. Tomorrow would be a long day.

CHAPTER **10**

PEOPLE STARTED gathering around Capernaum late in the morning. Some came early to sightsee, others as part of their vacation, the bulk just for the meeting that afternoon. Aaron had business to attend to in Nazareth, so Joshua and Aaron's family had the thrill of riding in a military vehicle.

Joshua walked among the people who were already gathering for the occasion. He seemed so ordinary, so casual, without the slightest air of self-importance, that it was easy to overlook him, and so he fast became lost in the crowd. By afternoon, Aaron had everything organized to the last detail, and committee members were ushering people to the area outside the city where the event was to take place. Joshua smiled. It was not the first important sermon preached on this hillside.

At two o'clock the program started. People were sitting all over the hillside, which was in an isolated area, the ancient Tabgha, which sloped gently along the lake, providing the effect of a theater setting. It was quiet and peaceful overlooking the golden wheat field at the foot of the hill and the calm waters of the huge lake shimmering in the sunlight.

People had come from all over the land: from the hill country near Lake Huleh, and from Haifa and Mount Carmel, from Nazareth and Tsipori, from Nablus and

Ramallah, and many from Jerusalem, and a large contingent from Bethlehem and the surrounding hill country. Desert people were also there, invited by Sheik Ibrahim. There were Jews and Arabs and Christians of all descriptions. And not to be forgotten, the two shadows who had followed Joshua everywhere. They arrived at Capernaum in a van with eight others who spread out and mingled with the crowd. Susan was the first to notice them and alerted Aaron, who made a mental note of their presence.

Joshua asked Aaron if he would have the people settle on the ground in groups of about fifty or a hundred so he could walk through the crowd afterward and talk to the small groups while they were eating their lunch.

The organizers stayed on the lower area, with the idea that the sound would rise more easily, and they could be heard without raising their voices, as they had only the battery-run speaker system hooked up to a truck. Daniel Sharon estimated there must have been between three and five thousand people. Never in their wildest dreams did they imagine anything like this could happen.

Daniel was the first to speak, and as he approached the microphone, he was overcome with emotion, and tears flowed freely down his cheeks. He looked at Joshua and it all dawned on him. Daniel had read the Gospels as a college student and it then seemed so idyllic, so simplistic and unrealistic. Now he saw it all happening before his eyes. It seemed like a dream. When he looked over at Joshua and saw him standing there, he knew. The Gospel story was being relived all over again and it was still so idyllic, so simplistic and so unrealistic, but it was happening, and so the tears.

It took him a while to compose himself, and then he began, "My brothers and sisters, never would I have dreamed that I would be addressing in my lifetime an audience like this, of Arabs, Jews and Christians, and calling them all brothers and sisters. Even a few weeks ago, if anyone had told me this could happen, I would have laughed at them. But we are here and it is so beautiful. I would like to start our simple program this afternoon with a song. We are privileged to have with us today an unusual man. He spends his life bringing love and joy into others' lives with his music and his friendliness. Many Arabs and Christians as well as Jews already know him, for he travels from village to village just loving people and hugging them and playing music for them. His name is Shlomo.

As soon as his name was mentioned, everyone seemed to know him, and a thunderous applause arose from the crowd. Shlomo arose and approached the microphone with his guitar. "The song I would like to sing for you today is one I composed last night after Daniel Sharon told me I had to come here. He didn't know that I intended to come anyway. The song God inspired me to write down is named "In God's Family There Are No Strangers." I will play it once and sing it, then I would like all of you to hum it the second time. The third time around I would like everyone to sing together, loudly and clearly."

With that he began his song. It indeed was inspired.

In God's Family there are no strangers,
Only brothers and sisters.
We walk down each other's streets and never say "hello."
We pass each other's houses and never stop to visit.
We hurt and pain and wound each other,
So often without cause, not even knowing why.

In God's Family there are no strangers,
Only brothers and sisters.
But today, things are different.
We have all found our Father,
And we are no longer strangers.
A new life has sprung among us, a new day has dawned.

A new hope has arisen,
Because in God's Family there are no strangers,
Only brothers and sisters.
And we are one and we are one, ever more only one.

When Shlomo finished, Daniel thanked him, then introduced Aaron, who was also deeply moved by the sight of all
these different people on a hillside by the Sea of Galilee.
He thanked everyone for their sacrifices in making not only
the long journey to Galilee, but the long journey in faith
and trust in one another to make this day possible. He finished by introducing Susan, who was one of the original
organizers of the group. He apologized to the more funda-
mental Arab people present, but since Susan was the
dreamer who helped initiate this whole program, he felt it
would be wrong not to allow her to take her rightful place at
this assembly. He then introduced Susan. Almost everyone
applauded.

"My dear friends," she began, "and I know now that we
are friends, I will not take much time, because I know why
you are all here. It is not because of me, nor is it because of
anything any of us has done. It is because of one man, a
man who was, until a few weeks ago, a total stranger. Even
today none of us knows very much about him, but we have
all come to love him dearly. No one even knows where he
lives. Indeed he seems to have no place to lay his head, and
I find myself lying in bed at night worrying about him, wondering under what tree he sleeps and on what hillside.
Many of you have already met him, not just at our meetings,
but as he walked through your villages, quietly, lovingly,
touching your sick and your troubled. I know for certain
the lives of many have been changed by his touch, as well as
by his words. When I first met him, I thought he was a simple man. As each day passes, I see his beautiful life unfold-

ing and realize that in our midst is a person who has been sent to us, I feel, for only a brief moment, to pass through our midst as one of us, but as one who carries in his soul the brilliance of God's own light, and the passion of God's own love, to show our blinded minds a new way, and our sick hearts a new love, to make it possible for all of us to dream a new dream of a future together as indeed a new family of God, sharing a common purpose to build a whole new nation together and show to the world how beautiful it can be for brothers and sisters to live together in harmony. This man I now present to you. Joshua, please come forward."

Joshua approached the microphone with a serene smile and a casual demeanor and looked across the crowd. It was so familiar. As of old, "he felt sorry for the people, they were like sheep without a shepherd." Looking at a small group with crutches and walkers, he addressed the crowd:

"We have come here battered and bruised and hurting, not because of something God has done, but because of what we have done to one another. I saw two little children this morning. One was blind and the other was crippled. They were playing together and laughing and having fun, as children should. One was an Arab, the other a Jew, but they didn't know that, they were friends. The Arab child had been shot in the head by a soldier's bullet, the Jewish child wounded by a terrorist's grenade. But they were too small to know hatred, and vengeance was still foreign to them. They were just friends playing together and sharing their cookies and candy.

"It has been said, 'You shall not kill,' but I tell you, evil does not begin with the soldier's bullet, or coward's grenade. Evil is conceived in the human heart. That is the great sin, because it assaults the temple of God's presence within one's soul and drives God from that soul. In the hate-filled heart Satan makes his home, because hatred is the foul air where Satan thrives. It is the nourishment of

sick minds. Satan cannot exist where there is love. If someone asks me, 'Is my child possessed by the devil?' I will ask
that person, 'Have you taught your child love?' In that you
have your answer.

"I can see so many of you have heavy hearts, and so many
worries. Stop worrying. Look at the world around you, the
warm sun, the vast blue sky, the air so fresh and clean, the
water teeming with life, and the wheat ready for the harvest. It is all yours, it is the expression of God's love for
you. Look at that flock of swallows. They are so free. They
don't worry about their next meal. They don't worry about
the winter. Your heavenly Father cares for them. You are
worth more than all the flocks of birds and all you do is
worry, as if you never had a heavenly Father to care for you.
Stop worrying. He is more like a mother than a father and
looks over you not to find fault or to accuse, but with tender
love. Indeed, call Him 'Abba,' 'Daddy,' because that is what
He is to you. He will care for you, He will heal your
wounds if you give Him a chance. He will prepare you for
the future. You are concerned with tragedy. There will
always be tragedy. That does not come from God, but when
tragedy strikes, He is closer than ever because He knows
you need Him. And in His home all wounds are healed and
all pain is taken away, and there the joy and peace is endless. So do not be afraid of those who can kill the body, but
only of those who can destroy the soul, because when the
body dies a new and more beautiful life begins. I know
because I came from there, and I have seen what my Father
has prepared for those who love Him."

The vast crowd, spread out across the hillside, sat there
spellbound, hanging on every word, many with tears in
their eyes, and filled with a peace they had never known
before.

When Joshua finished, the whole crowd rose and
applauded wildly. That wasn't what he was looking for, but

he accepted it as a spontaneous expression of their appreciation for what he had given them, something they had been starving for all their lives and had never received.

The crowd eventually settled down, and Daniel spoke to them, giving them instructions for the next item on the agenda, which was lunch. Joshua had spoken for well over an hour, and the crowd was hungry. While they ate, Joshua walked among them, talking to them in small groups, families pouring their hearts out to him with problems plaguing them, others asking him to pray for them, others asking him to touch their little children and bless them, just as of old.

Susan had been trying to get his attention, because he had forgotten to eat, and she thought he must be hungry and tired after that long talk. She ended up bringing lunch to him, so he could eat it while he moved among the people.

Father Ambrose Boyd was there with a group of his friends, including three Orthodox priests. Rabbi Herbstman and his wife were also with him, as well as Father Elias Friedman, all having a good time. In the group next to them were a dozen Protestant Pentecostals who had heard of Joshua's reputation and were anxious to meet him and hear him speak.

Joshua moved unobtrusively toward the men who had been following him all over the land and did not let on he had the slightest idea he knew who they were. They looked sheepish as he approached and asked them their names and what city they were from, and about their families. They answered briefly and gave no more information than was absolutely necessary. People around them sensed they were strange, but Joshua did not betray them.

During lunch Shlomo played the guitar and sang a medley of songs for the crowd. Some they knew and sang along with him.

After lunch, Aaron spoke of the practical steps the group might take to promote peace. One of the steps was writing letters to the officials of opposing sides and telling them strongly how they felt and how important it was that they take definite steps toward peace. They should also encourage their friends to become part of the movement, and if possible to attend the next meeting, which would be held on the hill outside Bethlehem. The date was set for that meeting and everyone was welcome and encouraged to come. Joshua then spoke for a few minutes, and the crowd departed. It was a totally successful day. Daniel, Aaron, Susan, and the others on the committee were beside themselves with how well Joshua's message was received and how friendly everyone was toward one another. Sheik Ibrahim came up to Joshua afterward and thanked him in the name of his family and said he had never felt such peace in his heart in all his life. He asked Joshua if sometime they could all meet on the Temple Mount. If he was willing, the sheik would talk to his friends in charge of the mosque and other leaders of the Arabic community and pave the way. Joshua thought that would be a splendid idea, since it was happening so spontaneously.

By six o'clock the hillside was empty, and perfectly clean. Aaron and his comrades decided to stop off with Joshua at a restaurant and have a little something to eat before they made the journey back to Jerusalem. It turned into a quiet but happy celebration.

11

ONCE BACK in Jerusalem, Aaron insisted Joshua spend the evening at his house. It did not take much persuasion as they were all tired from the journey. The children were told to get ready for bed. They asked Joshua to tuck them in and tell them a story, but they were sound asleep before he finished.

Aaron and Esther stayed up late talking to Joshua, sipping cordials as they relived the events in Galilee earlier in the day.

"Joshua," Aaron started, "I can't get over the ease with which you handled such a tense and suspicious crowd. Weren't you nervous?"

"What was there to be nervous about?" Joshua replied. "Everyone there came for the same purpose, with the hope that this time, perhaps, they might set out on a solid path to peace. People are sick of war, of hatred, and of living under siege. They feel guilty they can't give something better to their children than guns and bitter memories that poison their future. They came ready to listen."

"How do you think they left?" Esther asked. "People have been so disillusioned in the past and are so tired of empty words and promises that it is hard to imagine them being optimistic about anything. I know they felt good after your talk. So many told me of the peace they felt when you were speaking. They said they had never felt that way before. Do you think it will last?"

"With God's grace," Joshua answered, "and our continuing efforts, we can forge a way to peace. But Esther, remember, peace is a full-time job. It doesn't just happen. People's minds must be conditioned to thinking peace. That is what is difficult. Anger stirs up suspicions and fosters isolation. That isolation sends out messages, such as 'I don't want to have anything more to do with you,' which is itself offensive because it affects the innocent as well as the guilty and generates more hostility. So we have to keep people talking and encourage them to make the effort to be friendly. Friendliness also feeds off itself and generates corresponding good feelings. Peace cannot grow in a vacuum. A climate of peace must be cultivated.

"And it has to start with the children. It is a terrible evil to teach children to be suspicious and to hate. Our people have to put past evils behind them and look afresh to the future. Their children have a right to be happy, and they have a chance only if parents don't instill their own hatred and prejudice in their minds. Every child should be allowed to start life free of suspicion and with a happy outlook. So, yes, I think what people found today will have a lasting effect, if we keep up our own efforts and pray."

"Why do you say 'pray'?" Aaron asked, with an almost cynical grin. "I never saw much value in praying. I've seen too damn much of it in pious people who use it as a mask for meanness."

"Come now, Aaron, you know not everyone is like that," Joshua replied with disappointment in his voice but fully appreciating Aaron's past unpleasant experiences. "God has the same problem you have with people. But real prayer is valuable. It is inviting God into your life and sharing your life with Him, and even more important, listening to Him as He guides you. When prayer is sincere, God listens, and

He can move hearts just as easily as He can cause the wheat to grow and the trees to bear fruit. With His help our task will be much easier. Without His help an army of psychiatrists could not change these people's hearts. Do you think that what happened in Russia was just an accident? Mikhail Gorbachev came from a prayerful family. On the backs of the pictures of Lenin and Stalin in his family's living room were icons of Jesus and Mary. He is a man of deep faith, and knew he had a destiny from God to lead his people to freedom. In six months he dismantled an empire which had stood for seventy-five years. And he did it peacefully."

"How do you know that?" Aaron asked impetuously, thinking he had finally caught Joshua off guard and was about to trap him into revealing something about himself.

"It is easy to pick up information these days with communication being so instantaneous," Joshua responded. "Gorbachev himself told the priests who arranged for him to meet the pope that he had a faith which he got from his mother. He also told them he knew he had a destiny that would not fail."

"You mentioned Jesus," Aaron said. "Do you believe in him?"

"Aaron, how can a Jew not see beauty in him? He is part of our history. His life and goodness reflected Yahweh's presence in a way that is unparalleled in all of our history. What others have done to His message does not diminish his beauty or his greatness. Our people should be proud he is one of us.

"Joshua," Esther said, "when I was watching you speak to that crowd today, I have to tell you, you reminded me of the stories I heard about Jesus. And I thought he couldn't have been much different. Even the setting was striking in its similarity."

"Well, I'm tired," Aaron finally admitted, "and unlike you two, I have to work tomorrow."

"Chauvinist!" Esther shot at him as he picked up the glasses and headed for the kitchen.

They were all tired. It was almost two o'clock, the edge of a new day.

The children beat the alarm clock and woke everyone early. The first thing they did was look for Joshua to finish the story for them. They knocked on his door and pushed it open. Joshua was on his knees facing the open window, deep in prayer. He didn't hear the children. They discreetly tiptoed back out and closed the door quietly.

"Abba, Daddy," the little one said as she entered her father's room. "Joshua is on his knees praying."

"How do you know that, little one?" Aaron asked.

"Because we saw him," David answered. "We went into his room to ask him to finish the story he started last night. But we didn't disturb him. We walked back out and closed the door. He didn't even know we were there."

At the breakfast table, the two little children fought to sit next to Joshua. Who could deny them? They made him promise to finish the story after breakfast.

Esther passed around the bowl of fresh figs. "I know they're not quite in season, but we got some from friends back from vacation."

Joshua immediately thought of the fig tree on the road to Jerusalem from Bethany, the one he cursed because it looked so promising but bore no fruit.

After breakfast Joshua took the three children out in the yard and finished the story.

"Last night I told you about the very special donkey. He was just an ordinary donkey, like all children are ordinary, but he had a special job, just like each of you will have a very special job to do when you get older. I told you about how this donkey was trained for his very special job and then one day he was sold to a holy man called a prophet. From then on the donkey used to carry the prophet everywhere. Sometimes the prophet would fall asleep on the journey. Any other donkey would have stopped to graze or to lie down, but not this donkey. He continued on the journey and when the prophet woke up he found himself just where he wanted to go. But how did the donkey know? Can you tell me that, David?"

The little boy shook his head.

"After many years, the donkey grew old, but still he carried the holy man wherever he wished. But the prophet was growing old, too. And on one journey, while they were traveling along a deserted road, the prophet became ill, and falling forward, rested his head on the donkey's neck.

"The donkey knew the old man was sick, and what do you think he did? He walked off the road and took a very dangerous path through a valley and hills that sheltered robbers and thieves. However, the donkey was smart, and he cared for the burden on his back, so he cleverly took a path that circled around behind where the bandits usually waited in the rocky hills and avoided them.

"Not far from the hills was a village where a kind old doctor lived. The donkey was born in that village and, though he never talked to anyone, he knew things about everyone there. He remembered just where the doctor lived and carried his friend to the door of the doctor's house and banged on the door with his hoof until the doctor answered.

"After lifting the old prophet from the donkey's back, the doctor carried him into his house and examined him and put him in bed. After a few days under the doctor's watchful care, the prophet regained his strength and was able to continue on his journey.

"No one even realized what the donkey had done, and no one even thought to thank him. He could tell no one about it, and no one ever knew how the old prophet found his way to the village and the doctor's house. But the donkey didn't care whether anyone knew or not. He loved the old prophet and needed no thanks and no applause. He was simply glad he was able to save his friend's life.

"When you get older, perhaps the most important accomplishments of your life may go unnoticed or unappreciated, but that's all right. You didn't do them to be appreciated, or to be noticed. You did them for God from the goodness of your heart, to brighten other people's lives or to make the world a better place to live in. And that is what will always make you precious in God's eyes."

"Joshua," David asked, "if no one knew about the donkey's story, how did you find out?"

Joshua laughed loudly, surprised at the child's sharp mind, and told them someday they would understand.

When Aaron left for work, Joshua asked if he would drop him off in the city. The kids didn't want him to leave. He hugged them and said good-bye.

No sooner had Aaron left Joshua on the street than the two intelligence people picked up his trail again. It was a mystery how they knew where to find him. And just as surely, an Arab boy was not too far off, always in the crowd, and always pushing his bicycle should he need it. The two boys now took turns watching out for Joshua, so it didn't look obvious they were following someone.

If the men thought they were going to follow Joshua this day, they had another thought coming. Joshua spotted an Arab riding a camel. Sensing the man was headed in the direction he was going, he asked him for a ride.

"I'm going to Jericho," the man said.

"I know. That's where I'm going," Joshua responded. "Would you kindly give me a ride?"

"I'd be happy to," the man said.

As the man nudged the camel to sit, Joshua mounted and the two men rode off, to the utter despair of the two agents. The boy laughed to himself, seeing how upset the men were. But it didn't take them long to recoup, and in a mat-

ter of minutes a military vehicle appeared. The men board-
ed and tried to catch up with the camel. It had disappeared, vanished like a puff of smoke. Where could they
have gone? There was nothing along the highway on either
side. Driving farther down the road into the valley, they
found the camel again, but there was only one man riding it.
Joshua was gone.

Joshua had asked the man if he would drop him off in the
desert, so he could walk to the hills; the man obliged him.
Joshua immediately set out for the rocky cliffs overlooking
Jericho. The boy had followed along the road on his bicycle
to where the highway opened onto a wide stretch of desert
where the boy had no cover. However, he knew the men
had only one way back to the city and that was this same
road, so the boy climbed up on the rocks and just waited.
He could see the vehicle in the distance and the camel as
well. A long way off to the left he spotted a lone figure
crossing the desert. It had to be Joshua. The boy chuckled
at his uncanny shrewdness.

The men in the vehicle questioned the camel driver for a
long time, apparently getting nothing from him, because
they turned back and tried to find tracks on either side of
the highway. By now the boy could see Joshua was a good
distance into the foothills. There would be no way they
could catch up with him. The men finally decided he had
gone in that direction but it was futile to try to follow him,
so they turned back to the city, no doubt to report to headquarters and let their superiors decide what to do. They at
least knew where their man was, and they could catch up
with him at any time.

The boy followed the vehicle until it reached headquarters.

That night Joshua spent in the caves on the side of the
rocky escarpment. Here was the place where he retreated

long ago to prepare for his ministry. Here was the place where he was tempted by Satan. The site was totally barren and empty of life other than a few animals and birds who made their homes in the rocks.

Walking along a narrow ledge for almost five hundred feet, Joshua had found a cave and entered. It was the same cave where long ago he had spent forty days and nights fasting and praying. This time, too, he spent the night praying. As the sun was setting, Joshua could see for miles, far across to the city of Jericho, and down along the northern end of the Dead Sea.

The events that took place there were so real. The blind beggar by the roadside crying out, "Jesus, Son of David, have mercy on me," and jumping up and down like a child when he saw the light of day for the first time; and the diminutive chief publican, climbing out on the branch of the sycamore tree so he could see Jesus when he passed by, and his delight when Jesus stopped and called him by name and invited himself to his house for supper.

The next morning on waking up, he got up and looked out across the valley. The sun was rising and turning everything a reddish gold hue. In imagination Joshua could see all the kingdoms of the earth Satan had promised for one act of devil worship. He could also see the loaf-shaped rocks the devil tried to nudge him into miraculously turning into loaves of bread, but to no avail. In the dark of night Joshua prayed for all his new friends, and for peace.

It wasn't until the next day the two intelligence men with four others left headquarters and started out after Joshua. This time the Arab boy was ready. He had a motorized bicycle. He also brought lunch, a pair of binoculars, and a two-way radio to contact a contingent of friends whom he had mobilized in case the men should try to do something to Joshua. The boy sensed a drama was about to unfold.

The men scoured the hills for almost four hours. The Arab boy spotted Joshua nearby as he was approaching the highway. The boy laughed to himself. Joshua had eluded them again and would be well on his way into the city before the men could catch up with him. This simple man was making a fool out of these intelligence people. It was as if he knew beforehand every move they would make and adroitly sidestepped them, leaving them wringing their hands in frustration. The boys relayed brief, cryptic messages to one another, telling each one along the way what had happened, then signed off.

Joshua was aware of the boy's presence but betrayed no sign of recognition. He did not go back to Jerusalem, but headed up into the hills and worked his way to Ein Kerem. Even though the land had changed over the centuries, Joshua remembered every road and pathway and had no difficulty finding the village.

Ein Kerem was an ancient town tracing its origins far into the Bronze Age. In the time of Jesus, it was where John the Baptist was born and grew up. It was roughly five miles from Jerusalem, in the Judean hill country, not far from the main government buildings in Jerusalem. Ein Kerem was also the place where Mary visited her elderly cousin Elizabeth, already six months pregnant, and felt her child leap within her at the approach of the mother of her Lord. Mary was at the time herself only a few weeks pregnant. For centuries Ein Kerem had been inhabited by Muslims and Arab Christians. Recently they have been replaced by Jewish settlements.

Joshua walked through the town, remembering the ancient sites, and visiting familiar places like the church which sheltered the remains of Zachary and Elizabeth's house. His real purpose in coming there, however, was not to sightsee but to visit close friends of Aaron and his companions and interest them in his campaign for peace, a herculean task.

Joshua stayed for two days in the town, watching, waiting for the right moment and for the right person, much like his one-man invasion of Samaria long ago, when his contact was the disreputable woman at Jacob's Well who had been married five times. She became his emissary to the Samaritan community.

The day after his arrival, an incident occurred as Joshua was wandering through town. A truck came plowing down the main street when a child thoughtlessly chased a ball out into the street and was struck by the vehicle and thrown up on the sidewalk. Joshua witnessed the incident.

People, hearing the screeching brakes, began to converge on the scene. Two construction workers coming out of an alley were the first to reach the child lying there unconscious, her head covered with blood. Joshua calmly walked over and bent down, quietly caressing the girl's face and head with his hand, as if wiping away the blood. As he did so, the girl slowly opened her eyes and looked up at him. He arose and continued on his way, leaving the two men and the others just arriving to care for the girl.

Word spread of what had happened. Some said the girl was dead and this stranger brought her back to life. Others laughed at the idea and said she had only fainted. The two construction workers told the parents the bare details and left it up to them to believe what they wished. The fact that there was no trace of a wound when just a moment before the stranger touched her the girl's head had been covered with blood said all that needed to be said. Whatever had happened, their daughter was well. But the stranger was nowhere to be found.

It was the next day, as Joshua was sitting on a bench along a sidewalk in the shopping district, that a shopkeeper named Anna recognized him as the man who had healed the little girl.

"Aren't you the one who helped that little girl yesterday?" the woman asked.

"Yes," Joshua answered simply.

"Was she dead?" the woman continued, trying to solve the mystery.

"That is of little importance. She is well now. That is all that matters," Joshua replied politely.

"What did you do to heal her?" the woman persisted.

"I did nothing more than what you saw," Joshua responded.

The woman went back into her store and phoned the family of the little girl. They came up the street immediately and found Joshua still sitting on the bench, watching people as they went about their business, with such harried looks on their faces, seemingly beset with so many heavy burdens.

It was quiet time, and some stores were closed for the afternoon.

"Sir," the little girl's mother said to Joshua, "are you the one who helped our daughter?"

"I saw her lying there on the ground and I went to see if she was all right. She is all right, isn't she?" Joshua said simply.

"We know you are just being modest," the girl's father said. "Whatever you did, you gave our daughter back to us and there is no way we can adequately express our gratitude to you. Would you please honor us and come to our house? We would like our daughter to meet you. Oh, by the way, my name is Elias and this is my wife Sarah."

"Shalom," Joshua said in reply. "I am Joshua. Yes, I would like to meet your little girl."

Anna, the shopkeeper, who was just closing her store, came over to the three of them. Sarah turned to her and hugged her for being so thoughtful in calling her.

"Anna, thank you so much for finding this wonderful man for us. I'd given up hope of ever meeting him, as nobody seemed to know him. Won't you please come down to the house with us now that your store is closed?"

"Yes, I'd like to see Ada, she is such a lovable child. I'm so glad she is all right," Anna said, obviously delighted. The four of them walked down the street.

Elias and Sarah lived in a modest home, one of the older ones in town. When they entered, the little girl met them at the door.

"Joshua, here she is, here is our little Ada, whom you saved yesterday. Isn't she a beautiful child?" Sarah said as she ushered everyone into the living room.

"Ada, this is Joshua, the man who saved your life yesterday when you were hit by the truck," the mother told the girl.

Joshua reached out and rested his hand on the girl's head. She looked up into his eyes and smiled but did not recognize him.

After they all sat down, Sarah served refreshments.

"Joshua," Elias said, "since yesterday our phone has been ringing off the hook, people wanting to know who this stranger was who saved Ada's life. And we couldn't even tell them. We want you to know we will all be eternally grateful to you for your kindness. You must be very close to God. The two construction workers told us all the details. They certainly were impressed. They've already spread your fame thoughout the neighborhood. And even they couldn't tell people your name."

Joshua just laughed.

As much as the family pressed Joshua to tell them whether the girl was dead, Joshua would not answer. The rumor the two men spread around town was that the girl was so badly injured she had to be dead. You could tell her skull was cracked. There was no way she could have survived that blow.

All that Joshua was concerned about was that the girl was now all right, and everyone should be grateful to God for giving the child back to them.

Finally, the family pursued the matter no further, and

Sarah set about preparing for supper. They decided on an early meal to accommodate their guests. Anna had to get back to work, and Joshua had other things to do before the day ended.

By the middle of supper, Ada began to warm up to Joshua, though she still did not know what everyone was talking about, or what had happened to her. As she was sitting next to Joshua, he could talk to her quietly and at one point dipped a piece of bread into the sauce on his plate and gave it to the girl. After dinner he gave her part of his dessert. Now they were good friends.

Conversation during the meal centered mostly on Joshua, who he was, what he did for a living, where he came from. Joshua told them about his friends and the community that was forming among the Arab and Jewish people. Elias and Sarah were curious though not particularly interested, until he mentioned Aaron Bessmer's name. Then they brightened up and told Joshua they knew his relatives who lived not very far away, indeed, just down the street. In fact, Elias promised to call them after supper and see if they couldn't stop over afterward, if that was acceptable to Joshua.

Joshua's mentioning the involvement of military officers in their project seemed to bless it, and the others began to show more interest. Also since the movement seemed to mean so much to Joshua, they felt, out of gratitude, they should at least show some willingness to listen and, perhaps, even help in some limited way. Anna was very excited about the idea and said she would talk it up with all her customers, though she doubted if there would be much interest among those living in the settlements.

After supper, Anna left for her store. Elias called Aaron's relatives, Simon and Mildred Rose, who said they would be delighted to meet Joshua, about whom they had heard so much. They lived only two blocks away, in a simple dwelling like so many others in the settlement.

Although Aaron was not their favorite relative because of his close association with Arabs, they were all proud of him because he was a military hero and had brought honor and fame to the whole family. They were cordial mostly, however, because of their friendship with Elias and Sarah, who, like Mildred, belonged to the temple sisterhood.

After initial conversations, the topic came around to Aaron, since it bothered the family so much. "As for me," Mildred said, "I couldn't care less whether the Arabs even exist. I hope they drive them all out of the country."

"Mildred," Joshua said, "you are a religious woman, and you try to please God. Do you think it is pleasing to God for religious persons to harbor hatred for people of a different race or religion?"

"I don't know whether it is pleasing to God or not, but I know how I feel, and I can't forgive Aaron for what he is doing!"

"The ultimate judgment of God," Joshua answered, "will not be based on whether we are a chosen race or not, or on how we as Jews treat one another, but on how we treat all of God's children. If we say we love God whom we cannot see and turn a deaf ear to the desperate cries of anguish and deprivation all around us, we cannot expect God to welcome us into His home when we face Him on Judgment Day. Don't be too hard on Aaron. He and his family have gone through painful experiences that have brought him to where he is. He is merely trying to do his part to make life bearable for people. We can't continue living this way."

"You may be right, but everyone is filled with hatred around here," Mildred said, annoyed with this stranger preaching to her.

"That is precisely why it has to stop," Joshua said, pressing his point. "A community can't exist with everyone filled with hatred. That is what hell is. Your children deserve better than that. They have a right to grow free of suspicion and fear and hatred. We owe them that."

Mildred was not about to admit that Joshua was right, but she had to admit that he made sense.

"I take it you and Aaron are good friends and work together on this project," Mildred said.

"Yes, we have come a long way, and much goodwill has already been generated. You and Simon might even like to come to our next gathering to see what it is like," Joshua said with tongue in cheek, but serious nonetheless.

"Simon can go, but I really have no interest," she said.

"In fact, I think I might like to go," Simon interjected. "It will be good to see Aaron again anyway. We were always good friends. When do you meet next?"

"We will be meeting on the Temple Mount next Wednesday evening," Joshua answered.

"The Temple Mount?" Elias said, shocked. "You'll end up with a riot."

"No, it will be a beautiful event," Joshua replied. "Sheik Ibrahim Saud is making arrangements with the officials at the mosque for all of us to gather there. They have a great respect for the sheik. Don't you think that will be an event worth seeing?" Joshua ended by saying, not without a trace of humor.

They all agreed it would be extraordinary if it happened, although it was impossible to imagine something like that taking place.

As it was getting late, Elias, Sarah, and Joshua rose to leave. Even though the conversation was a bit heavy, it dealt with matters on everyone's mind, and in a friendly way, so it turned out to be a fruitful introduction for Joshua. He had accomplished his mission, with the help of fortuitous events and kind people, a beautiful example of the delicate way God brings people and events together to accomplish His carefully laid plans.

Joshua slept out in the fields that night. He had many things to discuss with his Father.

CHAPTER 12

THE NEXT day Joshua went up to Jerusalem. When he arrived, the city was in turmoil. A group of Arab students had been arrested and the Arab community was protesting. People were roaming the streets looking for trouble. As Joshua entered, Arab children were throwing stones at soldiers walking down the street. One of the soldiers turned his automatic rifle on the children, felling two of them. The others fled in panic.

Joshua rushed over to the children lying in the street. The soldiers came over and grabbed him, ordering him to leave. Joshua looked at them with anger flashing in his face, and said bitterly,

"You wouldn't have done this to your own. Why do you do it to these children? They are no less God's children than Jews. You will answer to God for this."

The soldiers were shocked and ashamed that one of their own would say that to them.

Joshua knelt down beside the children, and placing his head against their chests, listened for a heartbeat. There was none. Placing his hand on the children's heads, he prayed quietly. The soldiers, thinking he might be a doctor, just stood watching. An eerie silence hung over the empty streets. People peered furtively from their darkened windows. The soldiers, becoming nervous with the ominous silence, cast glances in every direction, as if expecting trouble, then looked down at Joshua and the children. They were stunned to see the children open their eyes and look up at Joshua. He took each of them by the hand and helped them sit up, then lifted them to their feet and told them to go home and behave themselves and keep out of further trouble.

The soldiers stood there in dumb silence, not knowing what to make of this odd Jew. Joshua looked at them in anger and walked away, leaving them standing there in the middle of the street. Arab people in houses adjacent to the street were now jeering at the soldiers, shouting "Shame! Shame!" for having shot little children. Many of the people, frightened by the noise in the street, had come to their windows just before the soldiers shot the children and had witnessed the whole incident. In a matter of minutes the episode spread like fire through the Arab community. When the soldiers reported the incident to headquarters, Aaron found out about it and couldn't wait to see Joshua and get the whole story straight from him.

Even though the soldiers did not know the man's name, Aaron knew it could only have been Joshua who would have done such a thing.

Joshua's popularity among the Arab community had now reached a new high. People were beginning to wonder who he really was. They knew he was a Jew, but the man clearly stood above the common herd of humanity by his sheer greatness of soul and manifested in his caring for people an uncommon sense of goodness that separated him from Jew and Arab and Christian yet made each of them feel he was a part of them.

Only those who had a stake in continuing the internecine conflicts were developing a hatred of Joshua that bordered on frenzy. Some people are so filled with hatred and need for vengeance that peace is like a poison that threatens to heal their tortured souls. That is the last thing they could even think of allowing. Joshua's effect alone on people of every description was capable, given the occasion and the time, of bringing about that peace. He seemed simple enough, but his simplicity was to these diseased minds a carefully calculated strategy to disarm the unwary and seduce people into thinking peace was possible. Merely bringing people to that state of thinking was a step toward peace. That could not be tolerated.

It was only two days later when this fact became very clear. Joshua had been visiting friends near the Pool of Siloam. He had dropped off some packages he thought the poor families in the area might need. Walking back up the hill above the pool, an isolated area, he was accosted by five men, Arabs. As he approached, they rushed him, pulling out knives, attempting to stab him. Joshua spotted them just in time and slipping behind a tree, picked up a large stick lying on the ground and fended off their attack, striking one of them in the head and jabbing another in the stomach, then knocking the knives from the hands of two of the others. He was then face-to-face with the last one, who lost his nerve when he was standing there alone with Joshua.

It was Sheik Ibrahim's son, Khalil.

What he could not accomplish with four accomplices, he was too cowardly to accomplish by himself. The majesty of Joshua's bearing awed him, and the look in Joshua's eyes was a look the man would never forget. It was a look of anger and a frightening threat of impending judgment, yet a look filled with an unbelievable compassion. In an instant it drained the strength and energy from the man. He turned, ashamed, and fled like a beaten dog.

The incident did not go unnoticed. Joshua's faithful young friend was watching from a distance and saw what had happened. That night he would have to report it all to his grandfather.

Joshua continued up the hill, using the stick to help him up the steep ascent. He was clearly troubled by what had just taken place, and his expression, which was ordinarily calm, became serious and distressed. The concern was not for himself. He knew he could control whatever situation might arise. His concern was for Khalil. He was not an evil man. He had been trained to hate from infancy. How could he not hate? Joshua could see clearly the fate that now awaited the man. The boy would tell his grandfather, the sheik, what had taken place. The grandfather would become enraged at the audacity of his son so flagrantly violating the family's honor and the sheik's orders concerning Joshua. The penalty for such an affront to authority was death by hanging.

Joshua spent the whole rest of the day preoccupied with the situation. That night he slept little. Far into the night he was still on his knees talking with his Father, asking His guidance. It was only a little before dawn when he finally lay down on the ground and, resting his head on the root of an ancient olive tree, fell into a deep sleep.

The next day he rose early and, after having breakfast at a little shop in the city, started out for the sheik's camp. Joshua knew the trial was already taking place while he was on his way, and by the time he would arrive, the young man would already have been convicted and condemned. Son or not, the family's honor and, what was more, the sheik's honor had been shamelessly violated. Such a crime could not be tolerated. As much as it broke the old man's heart to have to pass a sentence of death on his own son, it was his responsibility to his authority and to the tribe that he not cave in to sentimental feelings and fail to execute his duty to Allah and to his family. His son, his own flesh and blood, had attempted to assassinate not just someone who had become a dear friend of the family but one for whom the sheik himself had vowed protection and the enduring loyalty of his family. The shame and humiliation the sheik felt

over the perpetration of such a crime by his own son devastated the old man. There was no alternative. The son had
to die.

Joshua knew what the outcome would be. He hoped he
could bring some comfort to the family and mediate the crisis that had overtaken them.

Joshua arrived a little before noon. The atmosphere in
the camp was somber. People were gracious and wished
Joshua peace, but no one seemed happy. Even the children
who were normally jovial and in high spirits seemed
depressed and listless. They weren't even playing.

The sheik was in his tent. Joshua asked if he might see
him. Naturally, the answer was yes. Joshua had immediate
entree to the sheik whenever he should wish to see him.
Joshua entered the tent. The two men exchanged salaams
and the kiss of peace. Then, after the sheik gestured for
Joshua to be seated, they sat and immediately began sharing
with each other what was on their minds.

"My dear friend," the sheik began, "I cannot begin to tell
you how ashamed I am that you have been so insulted by
one of my family, and what is the greatest indignity, by my
own son. A thousand apologies, and I know that that is not
enough. I must tell you that we have just held court before
you arrived, and my son confessed his guilt. He will be executed tomorrow morning by hanging."

The old man was so ashamed that he found it difficult to
look directly at Joshua but forced himself to keep a steady
gaze. Joshua looked at him with no anger, or sense of insult,
but with a look of deep concern which was disconcerting for
Sheik Ibrahim.

"You do not look pleased, my brother, that I have decided
to execute my own son to offer satisfaction for what he
attempted to do to you," the sheik said, confused.

"Sheik Ibrahim," Joshua said calmly, "you have become a
beloved brother to me, and dearer to God than you could
imagine. I realize what the men tried to do yesterday. But

they could not hurt me. My Father would not allow it. Your
son's soul is eaten up with hatred. He was not born that
way, my good friend. He was taught to hate. He was merely being faithful and obedient to what he has been taught
since childhood. Because his teachers have changed as they
grew older does not mean that he will lay aside what was
instilled in him for a lifetime."

The sheik lowered his eyes in shame. He realized Joshua
was referring to him and the way he had brought up his son.
The sheik, as he grew older, had realized the futility of
hatred and vengeance and changed his whole outlook, especially since meeting Joshua, which confirmed his new vision
of life. But the son still carried on faithfully the lessons he
was taught.

Joshua went on, "To sentence your son to death is to
deny your son can be saved. No human being has the right
to terminate the life of one whom God has created. That
right belongs to God Himself. In days gone by, people pre-
sumed they had the right from God to destroy other human
beings, but my Father has given that right to no one. It
belongs to Himself alone. Your son, Sheik Ibrahim, is not
an evil man. If he can be exorcised of his hatred, he will do
much good, and one day you will be proud of him. I know
what plans God has in store for him. I beg you, my dear
friend, to grant me this request and spare his life, so God
may continue to work in his life."

The sheik was shaken by what Joshua said to him and felt
guilty that in condemning his son, he was condemning himself as well, because Khalil was a product of his teaching
and also of the sick environment in which they all lived.
There was a long silence. A ray of hope passed across the
sheik's mind at the possibility that he might not have to execute his son, but what about his own pride at rescinding his
order of execution? If it were someone else's son, he would
not back down. He would lose face with the rest of the
tribe if he pardoned his son. His people would never

respect him again. The sheik expressed these concerns to Joshua, who listened patiently and understood.

"Sheik Ibrahim," Joshua continued, pressing his plea, "if you pardon him, that is one thing. If I request you in front of your family, that is another thing."

"You would request me to pardon someone who attempted to assassinate you?" the sheik asked, the full import of Joshua's plea finally striking him. "That is difficult for me to understand. Forgiveness is not a virtue we are taught. You are so different from all of us, Joshua. Your ways are so beautiful. I wish I could have learned your ways from my youth. Our lives would be very different now. But how would you ask for this pardon?"

"I would ask that you assemble your family who are present here in the camp," Joshua replied. "You would then have your son brought before the whole family. I would at that point talk to your family, expressing to them my convictions and my feelings, and then present my request."

"Joshua," the sheik said, "I don't think I would do this for any other being alive. But since I have such respect for you, and since you are the person offended, I think it only right that I grant your request. I will call the family together immediately."

Getting up from his pillows with Joshua's help, the old man walked out of his tent and told his assistant to call the family together for a special meeting. Everyone was to come.

It was only a matter of minutes before everyone assembled. Last of all, Khalil, with hands bound behind his back, was led by two men into the front of the assembly. The sheik called for everyone's attention and introduced Joshua, who had asked to speak to the family.

Joshua rose and stood in the center of the huge semicircle. "My friends," he began, "I am no stranger to you anymore. I have been honored by Sheik Ibrahim in being made a member of your family. I know you are all aware of what happened yesterday. It is unfortunate. What your brother has done is not his fault alone. He lives, as do all of you, in a climate of hatred and revenge. It has become a way of life, and acceptable. But it is not God's way. It is not even reasonable. And it must come to an end if your people are to survive. Since I was the person offended yesterday, I have a right to express what I judge to be a legitimate request. I know your brother has been condemned. No matter what he has done he is still a child of God. No man has the right to take the life of God's children. It is the ultimate admission of despair, that there is no more hope for one whom God created out of infinite love. As long as God exists, there is always hope for even the most unfortunate of His children. It is for God to decide when He will take back the life He has given them. I know that my Father's work for your brother is not yet finished. He is to accomplish things that will one day make all of you proud. Now, he is a bound criminal condemned to die.

"I am aware of what the men attempted yesterday. They may have thought they were doing a good deed for a just cause. I do not agree. It is never a just cause to violate an innocent person. I do not approve of their evil deed. But I do forgive their sin, and I ask my Father as well to forgive them. And since the time is long past for us all to start forgiving one another if there is to be peace in this world, I ask my dear friend, Sheik Ibrahim, to pardon your brother so he may come to know God's forgiveness and find peace in his troubled soul. May God's peace be upon you all."

Finished, Joshua stepped back and waited for the sheik to respond. The crowd showed no emotion, just sat silently, intently. The sheik arose and walked over to Joshua.

"My people, my friend Joshua, my imam, I speak with a heavy heart, indeed, with a broken heart. What Joshua has said is true. We all share the guilt in the eyes of Allah. But evil must be punished. Joshua asks us to forgive. I must admit I do not understand this forgiveness. We have not been taught forgiveness. It is a strange teaching for all of us. But listening to Joshua speak I could see for the first time the beauty and the greatness of a man who can forgive. It makes him most Godlike. Khalil has committed a terrible evil. I cannot forgive him for that, though Joshua can find it in his heart to forgive him. Out of honor for Joshua who has already done so much, not just for our family, but for our people and for the cause of peace, I listened respectfully to his request to pardon the offender. While I cannot find it in my conscience to pardon such a heinous offense, I will change his sentence. The sentence of execution is revoked, but in its place, the offender will be banished from our family forever. He is not to be present in our midst, nor contact any of our family here present from henceforth. If he shows sorrow for his evil deeds and changes his ways, we will consider his situation at a time in the future to be determined by myself. The offender has one day to prepare for his departure. The meeting is over. The family is dismissed."

Khalil broke down sobbing like a baby. Still bound, he came over to Joshua and fell down on his knees, thanking him for his forgiveness, expressing his sorrow that he had such hatred in his heart, asking Joshua to pray to Allah to take the hatred from him. Joshua lifted him up and untied the straps that bound him. "Get up! You are forgiven. Be freed from the hatred that binds you!"

Khalil arose and looked into Joshua's eyes with gratitude and peace. Tears streamed down his face as he turned and walked away. The sheik watched from a distance, hoping he was witnessing a change in his son, then walked back into his tent with a heavy heart, thinking he would never see his son again.

Khalil was led back to his tent. A few friends came over to him expressing their relief and their sorrow for him. Most just ignored him. Joshua went to the sheik's tent and thanked him for his benevolence, then took his leave, promising that one day he would be proud of his son. As a

parting remark, the sheik assured Joshua that all arrangements had been made with his friends at the mosque for the
next meeting to take place on the mount. Joshua thanked
him, then left.

CHAPTER **13**

JOSHUA'S DEFT genius at avoiding unwanted intrusion into his privacy left the Mossad agents stunned and unable to account for his whereabouts over the previous twenty-four hours. Nor did they have the slightest clue as to where he was, or how he eluded them. So his reappearance in Jerusalem after leaving the sheik's camp was a further embarrassment. His disappearance not only intensified their suspicions and increased their own insecurity but put added pressure on their superiors to initiate some immediate action concerning him. There were no longer two agents assigned to track Joshua, but four. He, of course, was immediately aware of their change in tactics. He was also aware that the sheik had assigned two other grandsons to follow the agents, sensing some imminent and dramatic turn of events.

Indeed, Joshua's carefully laid plans were beginning to come together, and he was determined that nothing would frustrate what was so painstakingly planned. The scheduled meeting of Aaron's new "community" was to take place the following week. The Mossad had decided to execute their own plans concerning Joshua before then. Joshua was keenly aware of all the plotting, but he gave not the slightest hint that he had any idea of all the undercurrents. His ability to modify circumstances that threatened those plans became marvelously clear during the next few days.

Since the last meeting Aaron had appointed key leaders of small groups from various geographical areas and divided among them the list of all those who attended previous meetings, as a safe method of rapid and secure communication within the new organization. News of the upcoming meeting circulated in this way overnight; it would later prove to be an effective method of communicating with this vast group without using any of the news media, thereby avoiding unwanted attention and depriving obstructionists of an opportunity to create mischief.

That night Joshua met with his friends on Ben-Yehuda Street. They had not seen him in days and were excited when they spotted him walking down the street toward the cafe.

"Well, good friend," Aaron shouted as Joshua approached the table, "you certainly have a lot of explaining to do. It seems we can't leave you out of our sight for a minute without you getting into all kinds of predicaments."

Joshua just chuckled as he sat down next to Susan.

"Yes," Susan added, "and you have the Mossad agents tearing their hair out. We heard about you eluding them in the desert a few days ago. Even with the electronic surveillance equipment in their van they couldn't track you. You're uncanny. How did you avoid them?"

"And our own men at headquarters have been frantic over the incident with the Arab children," Aaron added. "What happened there anyway?"

"What did you hear?" Joshua asked him.

"We interrogated the soldiers involved. They were young fellows. It was the first assignment on patrol for one of them," Aaron said in an embarrassed attempt to excuse them, then continued, "When the Arab kids began to throw stones, he panicked. It's no excuse, and I'm ashamed, but more important, Joshua, what happened to the children?"

"They are all right," Joshua answered briefly.

"We know they are all right now," Nathan said, "but what condition were they in when you found them? We got two stories. The soldiers said they were slightly wounded. The Arab residents in the area said they were dead."

"Just thank God they are all right now," Joshua said, trying to pass over the subject.

"You are being evasive again, Joshua," Susan interjected. "Tell us what really happened. Even if the children were only wounded, after you touched them they got up and walked away with no trace of any wounds. Where were they hit?"

"They each had several wounds. It was an automatic," Joshua answered. "Why do you keep pressing? It should be obvious that God wants peace here and shows how interested He is in it by healing wounds."

Catching on to Joshua's ambiguous way of answering certain things, Simon broke in with the comment, "Well, I guess you just gave us our answer. You certainly have a subtle way of evading issues and couching facts. I can understand why the Mossad have a time with you. Not even their computers can figure you out. Talking to you is like playing a chess game. Every move is a maneuver."

Changing the subject, Aaron brought up the topic of the next meeting. The sheik had also informed him of the mosque officials' permission to use the square in front of the mosque for the meeting. They were at first concerned about the danger of a riot, but when the sheik assured them that there was no possibility of anything like that taking place, they accepted his judgment and gave their permission.

"How many do you think will be coming?" Aaron asked Joshua, as only he had a handle on the Arab community and their growing interest. Aaron also heard from his relatives in Ein Kerem that a good number of people from there would be coming as well.

"There should be quite a few more than last time," Joshua said confidently. "We are growing into a good-sized community."

"Of Jews, Moslems, and Christians," Susan said with ill-concealed pride. "Whoever would have dreamed of such a thing happening even a few months ago?"

"Yes, it is beautiful what can happen when people try to sense what God wants and open their hearts to His voice," Joshua said, making sure he got the point across as to who really deserved the credit for all the beautiful events taking place.

Aaron and Sheik Ibrahim had decided that the following Thursday would be the date for the upcoming meeting of the whole group. Extensive plans were not needed, though the mosque officials agreed with the sheik to set up an efficient sound system to accommodate the huge crowd that was expected.

Aaron wanted Rabbi Herbstman to meet the mosque officials in an attempt to prepare dialogues for the future. The rabbi was not only an intelligent man, he was bighearted and almost totally devoid of prejudice and racial or religious pettiness. Joshua also liked him and trusted him.

After talking a while longer, the group broke up. Knowing that the Mossad had plans, Joshua decided it was best for him to accept Aaron and Susan's invitation to stay with them for the next few days. In fact, even Nathan and Samuel invited him to stay at their places as well. This protected Joshua from the Mossad for at least twelve hours each day for the next week. So when they left the cafe, Aaron took Joshua home with him.

The next morning the children squealed with delight when they found that Joshua was in the house. During breakfast they vied to sit next to him, and after breakfast he had to play games with them, which he did until Aaron took him down to the city on his way to work.

In the city, Joshua was again trailed by the agents and the

ever-present Arab boys, who must have started out each morning tracking the agents as they left headquarters, because wherever the agents were, there were the children. They were dogged in their persistence and in their determination to let nothing happen to Joshua. He had by now become their hero. Still, Joshua never let on he had the slightest idea he was being followed, or knew what was going on, though he was aware of their every move.

During the next few days, he knew it would be safer if he spent the time in more heavily populated Arab neighborhoods, where the Mossad would have to be much more discreet. So he visited several of Sheik Ibrahim's relatives on the back streets of Jerusalem, one family in particular whom Joshua knew would ultimately play an important role in the community once the peace movement was well on its way. Their names were Majid and his mother Jamileh. They belonged to a respected and well-to-do family in the neighborhood. They were also good friends of another family that would play an important role in the peace movement, Elie, Soad, and Mathilde Zanbaghe, a brother and two sisters originally from Iran. Soad's husband, Siavosh Avari, was an engineer who had very well placed connections in the palace of the King of Saudi Arabia. Mathilde's husband, William, was also an engineer with other valuable contacts. Elie Zanbaghe was a genius at public relations and should have been a diplomat, but his most valuable asset at this time was his unique interest in the Jewish people and his rare insight into the complex issues facing the two hostile communities whose lives would be permanently and inextricably entangled. His feeling was that at some point they would all have to learn to get along with their neighbors if they wanted to thrive. They couldn't count on distant outside forces to protect them forever.

Joshua visited these people over the next three days and laid the groundwork for the roles they would be playing in the not too distant future. At their first encounter with him, they were impressed. They had heard of him from relatives. The sheik had previously contacted them to become involved, but they were not in town at the time. Now, having met Joshua and been told of the venture, they were enthusiastic to cooperate in whatever way they could. Joshua visited them during the day and later on met with Aaron and Susan and the others in the evening. He had already discounted events that were to happen the next week and was planning strategy for months down the line.

His vision was penetrating. He saw everything in very simple terms and refused to let human complications blur that vision. His steps were, accordingly, logical, methodical, and uncomplicated, like an artist who, with a few deft strokes, projects a powerful image on a piece of paper.

On Friday night, Aaron, Esther, Joshua, and the children went to the synagogue. Rabbi Herbstman had been invited to speak to their congregation, and Aaron thought Joshua would enjoy listening to him.

They arrived early, as Aaron wanted to introduce Joshua to his friends. Some had already heard of him. Surprisingly, a good number of Aaron's friends from military headquarters were present. Some were faithful attendants, but some came just for the occasion to hear Rabbi Herbstman.

The services were ordinary, except for the music. A guest musician from the United States, Joseph Eger, together with a few friends, provided the music for the ceremony. The rabbi was a thin man in his fifties, clean-shaven, with thinning and slightly graying hair and penetrating brown eyes. When he rose to speak, the sanctuary which was filled for the occasion fell completely silent.

"My dear friends," he began in a quiet, gentle voice, "I came across a strange man a few weeks ago on a Sabbath morning, walking through, or rather attempting to walk through, a Hasidic neighborhood in Tel Aviv. He was carrying a backpack and a canteen. As you can imagine, he might as well have been carrying a hand grenade, with the explosion that took place. Needless to say, he did not get very far, when I spotted him and extricated him from what could have been a tragic situation.

"It made me think, and I have done a great deal of thinking since then. So often we approach our religious situations from political or legal or cultural angles and will fight to the death over things that really have nothing to do with God. Even the Sabbath. Yahweh originally intended the Sabbath as a protection for slaves so that their owners could not work them to death. It was a day of rest and a time to have fun at family gatherings. It was religious leaders who thought that people were having too much fun on their day off and then turned the Sabbath into a legal nightmare, filled with endless prohibitions.

"What we have all lost in our religious focus, whether we are Jews, Moslems, or Christians, is how God feels about important issues in our lives. We have, in the course of our lives, deified our own political interests and prejudices, and even our own religions, so that God is no longer an entity to be even considered when we are making important judgments. We have effectively made Him irrelevant, because His values could too easily upset our carefully laid plans.

"We Jews worship God. Christians worship God. Moslems worship God. It is the same God, the same Intelligent Being. If He is alive and created us with tender love, then it seems only logical that He would want more than anything else that we love one another and would be delighted if we were to gather together and worship Him together. Yet what do we do—we kill one another, thinking we are doing God a service. But that is not the God for whom we are doing the service. We have made our religions and our cultural heritage God, and then kill in the name of that God whom we have created. It is the ultimate blasphemy.

"I saw a man last week playing a guitar. He was a Jew,

but he was playing his guitar and singing songs for a crowd of Arabs. They were dancing and singing with him as he played. I stood there with my mouth wide open in wonderment. "How beautiful!" I thought. And I cried, as I thought that God must be smiling. That was real religion, and I am sure God was pleased.

"What would be so evil for Jews and Moslems and Christians to gather together and pray to our God whom we all say we worship? I am sure it would please God if we were to find common goals and work together, and if we could plan our lives together, and work together as one people. Our ancestors lived in Spain for half a millennium under Islamic rule, and they treated us humanely. Why can't we treat their descendants humanely today? Why can't we live side by side in peace and prosperity and as one people work together for the common prosperity of our nation?

"There is someone here in our midst this evening. I say this not to embarrass him, but because he has touched my life and the lives of many others as well. He is also a Jew, but he wears a medallion given to him by an Arab sheik, who reveres him so much he has even asked him to be his family's imam. How unusual, how unorthodox, yet that wise old sheik has finally, in his old age, found a rare religious man who understands God and truly speaks in God's interest and in God's name. So, for that sheik, it was not unorthodox for him to want this Jew to be his imam. It was an honest admission that, after searching for a lifetime, he finally found God in the teachings of a very rare Jew.

"This Jewish man mingles so casually and so gently among Arabs and Jews and Christians alike. Of late we have been gathering by the thousands to be with him and to listen to him. He truly interprets for us the ways of God and in the beauty of his own life shows us how simple our life as a people can be if we can only learn to forget our past hatreds and suspicions and reach out to one another and find each other as children of God. It has to first happen among our own, whether we be Orthodox or Conservative or Reform or Hasidic. We have to be convinced that God is not pleased by the walls of hostility we build between ourselves. If we want to really practice God's religion, we must start by learning how in God's name to love one another. Then we can reach out to others and bring them into our sphere of love and concern."

Before he ended, the rabbi invited everyone to the Temple Mount the next Thursday to gather with the others for their scheduled meeting.

The congregation was quiet, not just during the sermon but afterward. It was a powerful message, but one that no one ever expected to hear in a synagogue. Joseph Eger, off to the side with the other musicians, repeatedly nodded his approval all during the talk and couldn't wait for the service to end so he could tell the rabbi how much he appreciated his words.

Joshua also smiled throughout the talk and congratulated the rabbi during the social afterward. Even Aaron felt good about religion that night.

The next few days were quiet days, pauses in the busy schedule of hectic meetings and personal encounters. Joshua's quiet time was not at night in the hills, but in secluded spots here and there in Arab neighborhoods. Whenever he wanted to be alone, he unobtrusively eluded the agents and could usually snatch an hour or two of privacy before they finally caught up with him. The Arab children, however, seemed to be more ubiquitous than the agents, and Joshua rarely escaped from their seemingly ever-present eyes. On one occasion, Joshua had found a secluded spot on the hill above the Hinnom Valley. The spot was shrewdly picked by Joshua. He reached it by walking up the hill through terraced alleyways between the houses of Arabs, where the Jewish agents would be most reluctant to follow. The children, however, had no such difficulty. The spot was near a Greek monastery. Joshua ate his lunch there and after resting knelt and, sitting back on his heels, folded his hands in his lap and for almost an hour was in deep thought. The children just watched him. At first, they did not know what to make of it; then they realized he was praying. He was totally absorbed. All they had ever witnessed were people praying in front of others on a prayer rug, or Jewish people at the Wailing Wall. Joshua's prayer was different. There were no body movements, no loud expressions, just total concentration and a beautiful peacefulness as if he were in the very presence of Allah Himself. The children were deeply impressed.

Thursday came around rapidly. People began gathering on the Temple Mount, or to the Arabs, Haram es-Sharif (the noble enclosure), at first timidly. This was forbidden territory for Jews. The officials of the mosque went out of their way, out of deference to Sheik Ibrahim, to make the visitors feel welcome. Indeed, Jewish people were the first ones to arrive, and they were most cordially welcomed by Muslim officials.

Aaron, Susan, Daniel Sharon, and the others arrived early to help with preparations. Sheik Ibrahim sent several of his lieutenants to help with whatever needed to be done. The sheik himself came just before the ceremonies were to start. With his advanced age, it was becoming difficult for him to travel and attend affairs like this. Joshua arrived in the midst of a large contingent from Tel Aviv and Galilee who had arrived by bus at almost the same time. He was already lost in the crowd.

The program started at two o'clock. The sheik was asked to offer a prayer at the beginning and say a few words. Standing before the microphone, dressed in white robe and Arab headgear, he appeared fragile. Though he was little more than five and a half feet tall, he looked tall and dignified. His white beard was neatly trimmed for the occasion. His green eyes carefully surveyed the vast crowd. More than eight thousand people almost half-filled the huge esplanade. The prayer the sheik offered was touching. The few words he said were simple but direct.

"My people, my friends, salaam! Shalom! This day is the dream of my old age. I have known poverty and I have known wealth. I have known love and I have known hatred. I have dreamed dreams and I have endured night-mares. I have seen children born and I have seen my children die. In the fading years of my life on this earth, I have learned much, but sadly, oh, so late. Had I in my youth the wisdom of my old age, I would have lived a different life. Hatred is an illusion. Hatred is the poison that destroys the dreams of innocence and turns the future into a living hell. It is the cancer that destroys our children.

"It is not like old men to talk about love. But only recently have I learned how to love. I have learned it from a Jew. I know he is a special person. He wandered from the desert into our camp one night and returned a lost lamb, my granddaughter's pet. He ate with us and stayed the evening with us. Wonderful things happened that night that changed my life. He taught us in a few hours how to love. Love is the answer to our problems here, not hatred, not revenge, but love. You can see what love has done for us all in just a few weeks. Look around you. We are Jews, Moslems, Christians, men, women, children, soldiers, politicians, even religious people. Look at where we meet, on this holy mount. This is the first time in all of human history that Jews and Muslims and Christians have met in this place together in the name of Allah, in the name of Yahweh, in the name of God. It is love that has brought us here. It is the work of God. What the future holds has to be bright, because God is our light and our inspiration. I may not live long, but being here today has given me hope for my children and for all our children. May God bless us all! Salaam! Shalom!"

After the sheik's words, Shlomo was asked to lead the group in singing as he did on the previous occasion. After the song, Aaron introduced Daniel Sharon, who spoke of the progress that had been made since the last meeting. The numbers had been growing steadily, and the influence of the group was beginning to be felt in high places. People had been asking what they could do in a practical way to create a better world. Daniel suggested that the purpose of the gatherings was not to tell people what they should do specifically, but to help people realize that there was much they could do, and that they should not be afraid to take whatever steps they felt inspired to take and attempt whatever good they were able to within their own circumstances and field of influence. They could contact their group leader if they had any questions. They in turn could always contact Aaron or Susan or one of Sheik Ibrahim's assistants.

Aaron and Susan then took their turns speaking, with Susan introducing Joshua. For some this was the first time they had seen Joshua, although they had heard so much about him. When he got up to speak, his appearance was disconcerting. He looked ordinary, but there was a dignity about his bearing that immediately set him off as someone very special.

"My friends," he began, "much has happened since our last gathering. God always makes things work for the good of those who love Him, and so many good things have happened to make this day possible. The goodness of the religious officials of this beautiful house of worship has made this gathering today memorable and historical. We are all deeply grateful to them for their kindness and their trust. It must please God very much to look down on what is happening here. And this is just the beginning.

"Cynics say it is impossible for our people to live together. From a human point of view, it may be true. But we forget there is a God, and a God who cares, a God who is the Father of us all and who loves us with the tenderness of a mother. It is His desire that we learn to find one another and reach out to one another in love and compassion.

"I saw a little Arab boy the other day run out into the street in front of a speeding car and pull a Jewish girl to safety. It was a beautiful sight seeing the two of them hugging and crying tears of joy. The families of those two children will be forever close.

"But walking through your streets day after day, I see so much pain, so much fear and anguish. Why are you so anxious? Why are you so afraid? Don't you know that God loves you and watches over you? I know you worry about your children. I know you worry about your jobs, and about your health. It is natural to worry, but it is of little value. You say God will not protect your children from a terrorist's bomb or a soldier's gun. You don't realize how many of your children God has protected from terrorists' and soldiers' guns and bombs. Had He not, many, many more would have died. Even those who died are at peace with Him, living a life of happiness you could never imagine. And they are still close to you, like the angels are to one another.

"Your Father in heaven wants you to enjoy the life He gave you here on earth. He has given you all you need to be happy. Much of the hurt and pain comes not from God, but from people's abuse of His gifts, especially free will. It is such a special gift, but one which ties God's hands, because He has more respect for the freedom He gave you than people do. Once given God does not take back. Freedom can so easily be misused and is so often used to hurt others. Injustice and meanness are not from God. God spends much of His existence picking up the pieces of broken humanity, caused by the meanness and cruelty of others, healing the hurt caused by selfishness. There is more healing in the world than you could even dream of. God channels His healing power through the gentle hands of caring doctors and nurses, but many wounds He heals Himself in the quiet of the unknown, where He touches your hearts and souls.

"Trust Him. He loves you tenderly. Do not be afraid to turn your lives over to His care. There are so many beautiful things God wants to accomplish through your lives. So let Him draw you into His life so He can work through you. Once you let Him into your hearts and learn to reach out to one another, and break the isolation that separates you, you will find peace, and in that peace find all the resources you need to provide lavishly for the needs of one another.

"If only you can learn to get along and help each other, and work together, this little country will become the showplace and the model for all the world; she will be the light unto the nations. The whole world will see how beautiful it is for brothers and sisters to live in harmony.

"The past has many hurts and injustices. As painful as it has been, it is the past. It must be forgotten. It is today that is important. And we must start now to create the climate for peace. Take your olive branches and wave them through your streets. Give them as tokens to one another. And learn to love. Let your leaders know your feelings. They are the obstacles to peace. They thrive on conflict. They cannot afford to have people love each other. They must know your sentiments and feel the pressure of your concern. From this day, know that you are God's children, brothers and sisters to one another. May God's peace reign in your hearts and may you be blessed in one another. Salaam, shalom!"

The vast group sat on the pavement all during the talk, in breathless silence, hanging on to every word that fell from Joshua's lips, reminiscent of times long past when on these very sites huge crowds gathered to hear him speak. When he finished, the crowd stood up and spontaneously applauded him, many people turning toward one another and hug-

ging and repeating Joshua's last words, "Salaam, shalom."
In no time the whole crowd was embracing people who
were complete strangers. The sheik walked up to Joshua
and embraced him, kissing him three times, saying to him,
"How beautiful, how beautiful, my son! God truly abides in
your soul and speaks through your lips. We are indeed
blessed."

Aaron waited until everyone settled down. Then after a
few final perfunctory ceremonies, and another song led by
Shlomo, the crowd was apprised of the next meeting and
told they would be informed as to its whereabouts. Until
then they were encouraged to initiate whatever gestures of
goodwill might inspire them and to pray for one another
and for peace.

In spite of the large numbers, the crowd dispersed in an
orderly fashion and left the esplanade spotless. Afterward,
Aaron and his colleagues met with the mosque officials and
introduced them to Rabbi Herbstman. They talked briefly
and made arrangements to have dinner together in the near
future. The officials had heard Joshua's talk and, when they
were introduced to him, told him how deeply touched they
were by the profound simplicity of his understanding of
God and wondered where he learned such beautiful sentiments.

In no time the mount was empty, except for a handful of
Arab people walking around and praying. In the distance
were the sheik's four grandsons, doggedly faithful to their
duty of watching over Joshua. Aaron, Susan, Daniel,
Nathan, Simon, and Sheik Ibrahim with his assistants
walked off together, with Joshua in their midst. The sheik
insisted they join him for supper at the Seven Arches. They
enthusiastically accepted.

That night Joshua spent at Nathan's. They lived out in
the country, in a large home. His family was very wealthy,
and everything in their house showed remarkably good

taste, the artwork, the furniture, the garden, and even the dishes. They kept kosher, and Joshua respected their attachment to the old ways, though his own life-style was far from traditional.

Nathan's parents were in their early seventies, warm people and sensitive. They showed a delicate respect for each other, which was not put on but quite natural and spontaneous. Joshua felt immediately comfortable in their presence. As it was late in the evening when Nathan brought Joshua home, they did not spend much time talking. Nathan showed Joshua to his room, and they all retired.

After breakfast, Nathan brought Joshua back into the city and dropped him off on Mount Scopus, where he visited the campus of the university. He had hardly arrived when the Mossad agents appeared, and far behind them on their bicycles at scattered intervals the Arab boys, always among other people. How the agents tracked Joshua's whereabouts was a mystery, whether through contacts on campus or from knowing he had stayed at Nathan's house the evening before and merely followed him to work the next morning.

When they arrived, Joshua was talking to a group of students. The agents, four of them this time, exited their van and walked up into the campus and surrounded Joshua, ordering the students to leave immediately. Grabbing Joshua, they marched him off to the van and promptly sped away.

One of the Arab boys saw what had happened and immediately alerted the other three on his portable phone.

"They have Joshua," Ali said. "I'm following close behind." Ali rode down the street past the campus's main entrance. The other boys caught up, and together they chased the van on its circuitous route through the city's heavy traffic. Around corners, down side streets, through alleys they went, and after almost thirty minutes of tortuous driving ended up in a sleazy part of town with poorly kept houses and odd-looking people. Parking the van in an alley, the agents dragged Joshua from the van, his hands tied behind his back, blindfolded. Entering the back entrance to an old house, the agents dragged him upstairs into a dirty old room with just a mattress, a few wooden chairs, and a lamp. Pushing him into the chair, two of the men left to check the rest of the building to make sure it was secure.

When they returned, they began interrogating Joshua. They asked him his true identity, where he had come from. As he had no identity papers, or papers of any kind, they were even more baffled. They tore the canteen off his shoulder and threw it in the corner of the room, then removed the blindfold.

Joshua refused to answer any of their questions.

"You have no right to touch me or question me. I have done nothing wrong."

"You will answer all the questions we ask either willingly or by whatever means we need to pry it out of you," one of the agents said, smacking Joshua across the face and pushing him against the back of the chair.

Joshua remained silent. One of the men slapped him again, as the other repeated the questions.

In the meantime, the Arab boys, realizing they were in a Jewish neighborhood, pulled yarmulkes from their pockets and put them on their heads. They had met down the street from the house where the agents had taken Joshua. Ali had already planned a strategy if something like this should occur. He decided not to tell his grandfather. It would be too upsetting for him. He sent two of the boys, instead, to Colonel Bessmer's office at military headquarters with all the details and with orders to give the colonel the phone number of Ali's portable phone.

Ali positioned himself across the street from the van, but before doing so he picked up two old nails and a chunk of broken glass lying in the gutter and stealthily worked his way into the alley and under the van, where he proceeded to push the nails into two of the van's tires and put the glass under a third, with the idea that there would most likely not be more than two spares inside. He then went across the street and three houses down and, sitting on a rock in a vacant lot, waited and watched, whittling a piece of wood to while away the time. The other boy, Mahmoud, sat on the steps of an old house up the street and started to read a paperback he had taken from his pocket.

Over an hour went by and nothing happened. No one left the building. The portable phone was ingenious. The small battery pack fit into the boys' pants, and the microphone and receiver were patched into their shirts so they could talk without holding anything in their hands.

Finally, Aaron called Ali. He was very upset but spoke in a calm, cool voice. "Ali, your friend here has just told me the story about you following Joshua and the agents. Where are you now?" Aaron asked.

"We are in a seedy part of town," Ali answered, and then described the section and the name of the street, as well as the house where Joshua was being kept.

"This is dangerous business you're in, Ali," Aaron warned him, "and I don't want anything to happen to any of you. So be careful! I'm sure you and your friends are all street smart, but be extra watchful now, because they are going to be on the lookout for anything suspicious. Act as if you are a part of the neighborhood. Don't appear to be too observant. I will have a special patrol sent down there to keep an eye on things. Don't give them any sign of recognition. If the Mossad make any move, inform me immediately."

"Colonel, I don't think they are going anyplace," Ali told him. "I put nails in two of their tires, and a sharp piece of glass under a third. They're stuck here, which means that one or two of them are going to have to leave on foot to get the tires repaired. That's over a mile away."

"Good job, Ali," Aaron responded, laughing loudly at his ingenuity. "You didn't tell your grandfather about this, did you?"

"No, he would be too upset. And he's an old man. It would hurt him."

"Good. Sit tight. My men will handle everything from here on. Should anything come up unexpectedly, call me immediately, and when they find out about the tires and take them away for repairs, let me know right away," Aaron said as a final instruction. Then, after giving Ali his special number, he hung up.

Inside the house the agents were still questioning Joshua, trying to pry out of him his full name, his place of birth, his reason for being in Israel, where he lived, who his family were, what were his reasons for meeting with Arabs and especially those who were suspect. Joshua, as on a similar occasion long ago, kept silent and answered not a word. This made the agents furious, and they began to beat him. His face was now full of blood, and he was retching violently from the blows to the stomach. Still, though tears flowed down his face, he spoke not a word, just gave them an icy stare.

Within an hour, a military jeep went by with four men in it. Shortly after, another jeep went by as if patrolling the neighborhood. The boys acted as if they knew nothing, but one of the soldiers, an officer, looked in Ali's direction and gave a slight gesture of recognition. Ali showed no reaction, just watched.

Every fifteen or twenty minutes the jeeps went by as if by routine. Almost two hours went by and still no action. Then, just before noon, two agents came out and entered the van. As they were backing out of the driveway, two of the tires popped, then the third. The van sank to the ground. The men got out of the van and looked at the tires and lost their cool. They let out a stream of foul language and then started to remove the tires. They had only one spare in the van. That they put on, but they had to take the others away to be repaired. As soon as the two men started rolling the tires down the street, Ali called Aaron. Within five minutes three jeeps came, filled with troops. Ali told the officer in charge they had taken Joshua up the back stairs of the house to the right of the van. Four of the men went up the back stairs, and four went up the front. The others stayed on guard.

They had no problem finding Joshua. His captors were shocked and tried to show their identification, but the soldiers acted as if they thought them just kidnappers, and as two soldiers held the agents at gunpoint, the others freed Joshua and led him out of the room and down the stairs to the jeeps outside.

Meanwhile, the soldiers on guard opened the hood of the van and disconnected the wires and the radio and were ready to leave when the rescue team appeared. They had to practically carry Joshua out of the house and into the officer's jeep, he was so crippled with pain. Then the contingent sped off.

Ali already had Aaron on the phone and was giving him a description of the operation as the soldiers pulled out. Aaron then told Ali and his friend to leave the neighborhood immediately, as if what had happened was of no concern to them.

By the time the soldiers arrived at Aaron's place, he was already there waiting for them, together with a doctor friend of his from headquarters, in case Joshua needed medical attention. They helped Joshua from the vehicle and led him into the house.

"Bring him into the bathroom, so we can clean him up," Aaron ordered. "Those brutal bastards will pay for this," he said in undisguised rage. "Did any of you recognize the agents?"

"No," was the unanimous answer.

"Well, I'll find out, and also who ordered it. They'll have hell to pay."

By the time Esther arrived, the only evidence of violence was the bloody towels lying all over the bathroom. Joshua was pretty well cleaned up. The doctor examined him. His face was red from the slapping, his nose was swollen, and his left eye was partially closed. Other than that, there were no signs of serious injury. But the doctor grimaced when he took hold of Joshua's hands to examine them and saw marks under the fingernails.

"What did they do, put needles under your fingernails?" the doctor asked Joshua, in a tone of disbelief.

Joshua looked at his fingers but said nothing. It would only incite more anger if he told them all the details.

"Those sadistic bastards!" the doctor said angrily.

"Do you want to lie down and rest?" Aaron asked Joshua.

"No, it's not necessary. There's no damage done, it's just painful," Joshua replied as they all moved into the living room. Aaron congratulated the soldiers on a masterful piece of work in rescuing Joshua and also praised the shrewdness of the Arab kids for the neat job they did. He then dismissed the soldiers.

"Well, it's certain now. From now on, Joshua goes nowhere without a bodyguard," Aaron said with strong determination.

Esther brought out a cup of hot tea and a couple of aspirin tablets, insisting that Joshua take them to ease the soreness.

"Thank you, Esther," he said as he took the tablets and washed them down with the tea.

"After you finish your tea, you are to go in and lie down and get some rest," Esther ordered. "I'll be your nurse, and I guarantee you will never have had such good care. I'll have you back in shape in no time at all."

"She's tough, Joshua," Aaron said, "but you couldn't have a better nurse."

After finishing the tea, Joshua did as ordered and went to bed. He almost fit into Aaron's khakis, a little baggy, but otherwise a pretty good fit. Aaron called the office and had two special army agents assigned to guard his house. When they arrived, he went back to work.

14

JOSHUA SLEPT through supper. Esther let him sleep, as he needed the rest to heal his bruised body. It was not until the next morning that he woke, surprised he had slept so long. The children were standing outside his door wondering if they would see him before they left for school. When they heard his footsteps, they were excited.

Joshua's face was bruised, and he had a black eye. The children felt sorry for him and hugged him, telling them how much they loved him and hoped he would be all right.

"Don't worry, little ones," he assured them, "I look worse than I really am. With your mother's good care, I'll be better than ever in no time."

"You're still alive," Aaron said to Joshua as he walked into the kitchen.

"Yes, thanks to you and all the others," Joshua replied.

Aaron could not help but laugh when he looked up from his paper and saw Joshua's black eye. Joshua laughed, too.

"It will go away in a few days," Joshua said good-naturedly. "At least I feel much better this morning. I am grateful to you and your men for what they did. They were soldiers at their best."

"The Arab boys made it easy," Aaron said. "They had everything under control. They really are street smart, those kids. They had been following you around for weeks, didn't you know it?"

"Yes, but I didn't let on," Joshua answered. "They really are sharp little kids. The sheik's trust in them was well placed. They did a good job."

As Joshua sat down at the table, Esther bent over and kissed him.

"That was a powerful cup of tea you gave me last night. I never slept so well or so long in my life," Joshua said to her.

"It wasn't the tea," she answered. "It was the beating you took from those hoodlums. Your body was in shock. But thank God, you look better this morning, except for your black eye."

After breakfast, the guards arrived to watch the house and protect Joshua. Aaron had already told the Arab boys that he would take over Joshua's security and they would not have to watch him any longer. The boys were somewhat disappointed but proud of their accomplishment and happy to be able to be kids again.

Aaron asked if Joshua wanted to come into the city with him, but he declined. During the day, he took walks through the neighborhood, talking to people. The guards followed him everywhere, always at a discreet distance out of respect for his privacy. Some of the neighbors knew Joshua from talking to Aaron and Esther. A few invited him into their homes for a cup of coffee and biscuits, though their real reason was to get acquainted with this stranger who had had such a remarkable effect on so many people's lives in so short a time.

The black eye and the swollen nose disappeared after a few days. By then Joshua could not wait to get started on his daily rounds. There was so much to be done.

Father Ambrose, the old Franciscan priest at the Church of the Holy Sepulcher, had been to all of Joshua's talks and had brought with him a host of friends of every description and religion. He had also met up with Father Elias Friedman, the Carmelite monk from Mount Carmel. The two had become good friends and had been corresponding. Joshua wanted to meet with some of these people again privately. So the first item on his agenda was the Franciscan monastery, and a visit with Father Ambrose.

The priest was at home and was excited when the doorkeeper told him there was a man named Joshua who would like to visit with him.

"Joshua, Joshua," the old priest said on entering the room. "How many times I have thought of you! How many times I had wished I could talk with you, but had no way of knowing where to find you. And here you are."

Father Ambrose grabbed both of Joshua's hands in his own and welcomed him cordially to their monastery.

Joshua was also glad to see him and told him how appreciative he was that the father brought all his friends to the meetings. "Father, you are a good shepherd. Your sheep are the kind of flock Jesus would have gathered around him, sheep of every description. It was good to see them in the crowd. I am also glad you got to meet Father Elias, the Carmelite. You have much in common. Help him; his life is not easy."

"Yes, my people were so happy they could hear your talks," Father Ambrose said. "You touched all of them deeply, even those who had been insisting they did not believe in God."

"I noticed that your friends come from different parts of the country," Joshua said. "Do you think you could encourage them to bring our message to others in their communities?"

"Joshua, they have already been doing that in a limited way. But I am sure they would be happy to do even more, especially if they knew that you requested it. By the way, my young friend, do you know there are two men following you? One of the friars noticed them as you were coming up the walk to the monastery."

"Yes, I am aware," Joshua replied. "Colonel Bessmer assigned them to protect me. A rather unfortunate incident occurred last week, and the colonel wanted to be sure I was protected in the future."

Since Joshua did not offer any further information, the priest did not pursue the matter, but asked him if he would like a tour of the monastery.

"Yes, I would like that." The old priest gave Joshua the grand tour of the spacious building. He was particularly proud of their chapel where the friars chanted their prayers and offered Mass every day. The tour ended in the refectory, the community dining room, where a few friars were sitting around a table, having a snack.

Father Ambrose pulled out a chair and told Joshua to be seated while he went to get the coffee and donuts from a nearby serving table. Sitting down, the two continued their conversation. Joshua made the priest feel his work in this world was not yet done, and even though he was on in age, the most important work of his life was about to begin.

After their snack, the priest brought Joshua over to the Church of the Holy Sepulcher for a relaxed visit to make up for his previous unpleasant experience at that sacred site. They did not stay long but passed through the church, taking a quick glance at the mementos of events long past.

When they finished, Joshua meandered over to Siloam to visit his friends, who were as usual tending their fields. He talked with them for a few minutes, bringing them up-to-date on happenings and in general letting them know he was thinking of them and hoped to see them all at the next meeting.

The next day a strange thing happened. A phone call came for Joshua at Aaron's house. Esther was the only one home at the time, and as Joshua was not there, the caller would not give his name, but said he would call back. That night he did call back. It was Khalil, the sheik's son. He wanted very much to talk to Joshua. Could he meet with him? After talking briefly, Joshua said he would meet with him the next day at the park on the east side of Jerusalem.

They met as planned. Khalil was already there when Joshua arrived. He was alone and sitting on a bench, sad and in deep thought. As Joshua approached, he arose and timidly extended his hand. They shook and sat down on the bench.

Seeing that the young man was on the verge of tears, Joshua put his hand on his shoulder in an attempt to steady him. Joshua was aware of the profound change that had taken place in the man's tortured soul.

As they sat there, Khalil unburdened his heavy heart, telling Joshua everything about his life, with a total confession of all the hateful things he had done even from his childhood. Joshua just listened.

"Joshua," Khalil said, "I have not slept since that morning in my father's camp. To be sentenced to death by your own father, when I had spent my whole life following the way he raised me, was a blow I could not bear. Then to be allowed to live but cut off from everyone I ever loved made the anguish all the more unbearable. And the realization that you could forgive me and even talk my father into letting me live has caused me nightmares. I have thought so often of suicide, then in the darkness of my tortured soul I would see your face, and the kindness in your eyes told me I was really forgiven, not just in words, but that you meant it and you really cared for me. I felt such peace. I was sure you were there by my side, so real I could touch you. Such peace and calmness I had never known before. You seemed to tell me I am not evil or worthless trash. I had the strange, eerie feeling that Allah was telling me He loved me. Gradually all the hatred and poison poured from my soul and your words at my father's camp came true, 'Go in peace, you are free.' Who are you, Joshua? So ordinary, so common, yet in your look and your touch I see and feel God."

Joshua just listened. When Khalil finished, he lifted his head and tried to look at Joshua. Tears streamed down his cheeks.

"You are precious to God, Khalil, and now that your soul is at peace, God will work great things through you," Joshua told him.

"What is it God wants me to do?" the young man asked.

"Don't worry about that now. What is important is that you open your heart to God. In time He will let you know what you are to do and you will have no doubt. In the meantime, enjoy the peace of being close to God, and let Him work in your soul healing you and teaching you new ways and a new understanding. He will put a new heart in you and a new vision."

"Joshua, I know what you are trying to accomplish. Can I be your disciple?" the young man pleaded.

"Yes, that you can be. But my Father has other work for you to do. Be patient and let Him speak to you in the quiet of your soul."

The darkness left the man's face, and a peaceful smile appeared. The two men stood up and embraced, Joshua resting the young man's head on his shoulder. Khalil thanked him for saving his soul and walked off.

Joshua stood there for a few moments, his eyes following the figure down the street as if following him into the future. A tear glistened in his eyes as he turned and walked up into the hills to enjoy the peaceful quiet of the warm afternoon.

Later that day he visited Sheik Ibrahim's camp and spent the next few days with him. The sheik was surprised but honored to see him. After supper the first night, Joshua and the sheik walked outside the camp for privacy and talked about many things. His son Khalil was forever on the sheik's mind.

"Joshua, have you seen my son, Khalil?" the sheik asked Joshua bluntly. "I worry so much about him. I stay awake nights wondering where he is and what he is doing, and if he is all right."

"Yes, my friend," Joshua said, "I have seen him. It was only this morning. Be at peace, your son is a changed man. You would be proud of him. Do not give up on him and do not stop loving him. My Father has beautiful things in store for your son. What had been twisted and tortured is now pure and innocent. He will be from now on an instrument of God. You can be proud. Understand why it is not wise to despair of any of God's children. God works in ways that are unfathomable to humans."

"Joshua, you have brought peace to my soul," the old man responded. "I cannot help but be responsible for what has happened to that boy. He was always a good boy and so very loyal to me. I think he loved me more than all the others. He was like a mirror of myself, and in condemning him, I knew I was condemning myself. He was everything I taught him."

"That is a problem parents have with their children," Joshua said. "They realize their mistakes too late, then flail themselves with guilt, rather than know that God understands their shortcomings and wants to help. He loves His children and will heal their deepest wounds and bring beautiful things out of the most twisted souls, if parents will only learn to trust Him to repair their mistakes. God's love is like snow on the mountain trails. In the fall the trail is filled with mud and dung from the passing of many animals. Then the snow falls, covering the tracks, and in the springtime the trail is filled with beautiful wildflowers."

"Joshua, you breathe such peace and goodness," the

sheik said. "I am an old man, and I have never met anyone like you in my long life. Thank you again for being a part of our family and for teaching us so many inspiring lessons."

15

THE NEXT meeting of the Children of Peace took place almost three weeks after Joshua's kidnapping. In the time between meetings, small groups were organizing throughout the land in Jewish and Arab communities. In some places the groups were mixed and even included Arab Christians of various denominations. Jews of every kind were represented, including quite a few Orthodox and a sprinkling of Hasidic Jews. Most of the Jews coming to the meetings were either Reform Jews or Jews who would not consider themselves religious. Father Ambrose's group was a motley assortment that met regularly at the monastery. The spirit and feeling among the people was so high that it generated enthusiasm among others in their communities, so that the groups were constantly growing in numbers.

Because of the large crowd expected, it was decided to hold the next meeting in an out-of-the-way place on the road down from Jerusalem to Jericho, just outside the city.

When the day arrived, people came in what looked like caravans of old, but with buses and cars and trucks rather than camels.

Aaron and Esther and their children took Joshua and Nathan along with them. On their way down to the site, Joshua's memory jumped across time and a smile crossed his face. Aaron, noticing the smile, remarked, "Joshua, what's the secret? Share it with the rest of us so we can enjoy it, too."

Joshua chuckled. "I can't share this one with you, Aaron. Coming down this road just brings back memories of long ago. It seemed like yesterday. I couldn't help but smile."

Nathan, who was sitting next to Joshua in the backseat, and was an avid reader of religious books, remarked quietly, "A man was going down the road from Jerusalem to Jericho and he fell among thieves . . ." then stopped and left the ball for Joshua to pick up.

Joshua turned, looked surprised, then smiled on noticing the impish grin on Nathan's face. Aaron thought Nathan was talking to himself and said nothing. As no one else in the car saw any connection, the matter was dropped.

As they drove along, all one could see was an endless train of cars and buses. People were flocking from all over. Approaching the field, Aaron commented about the good number who had already arrived and were busy greeting others as they came. Many had become friends over the past months and were glad to see each other, especially those who lived in faraway places. The group was melding nicely into a well-knit family. It was inspiring to see Moslems and Jews and Christians hugging one another, genuinely glad to see each other. Some even exchanged gifts and other tokens of friendship with people they had become particularly fond of.

Susan's genius for organizing was the key to the smooth running of the whole operation. She was at the site early with her assistants and already had matters well under control. She had thought of every possible eventuality, even the need for doctors or nurses in case of accident or a sudden illness.

Buses were now arriving from all over the Holy Land. Aaron and Susan, together with Jamileh and Charli and a few others, had spent days trying to find the right spot, with a large flat place for parking and a gently rising hillside so

the crowd could spread out. The place they found was a
natural amphitheater.

As the crowd was growing, a small contingent of Arabs
came walking from the parking lot over to where Joshua
was standing. They were young people, about thirty of
them in all, ranging from twenty to thirty years of age, not at
all like most of the people who came to the meetings.
These were tense, nervous fellows who could be intimidat-
ing, as if they had mischief up their sleeves. Many of them
looked out of place with their sullen, insecure expressions,
in contrast to the happy, enthusiastic air of the rest of the
crowd.

As they approached Joshua and the group he was talking
to, Joshua turned and looked at them, surprised and happy.
It was Khalil and his friends. Khalil beamed from ear to ear
as he embraced Joshua and introduced his friends to him.

"Joshua, these are my friends," he said. "I know they
don't look like much, but we have been together for a long
time and I talked them into coming to listen to you."

"Thank you, Khalil," Joshua said, as he shook the hand of
each of them and seemed to know each one's name, which
stunned them.

Joshua then introduced Khalil to those standing by, and
as Aaron and his friends were coming to get Joshua, he
introduced Khalil and his friends to them as well.

"This is Sheik Ibrahim's son, Khalil," he said to Aaron
and Susan, who were standing next to him. They gave them
a warm welcome and told them to feel at home and assured
them that everyone was a friend.

When most of the crowd had assembled, the program
started. It was much the same as the previous gatherings,
but people did not come to be entertained but to share
peace and goodwill and to hear Joshua's powerful messages.

Aaron introduced Soad Avari, a distant relative of the
sheik's, whose husband Siavosh was well connected in
Saudi Arabia. She was invited to speak out of respect for

the many members of her family who were represented in the group. Her family was totally committed to Joshua and was planning to take steps to make all Joshua's dreams practical. Soad spoke of the profound effect Joshua had had on their family and their whole community. If only there had been someone like Joshua among them years ago, the terrible tragedies of the present might never have taken place. What was needed was an entirely new way of looking at life and, indeed, a new understanding of God and how He relates to His human creatures. They had all been living as if there was no God, and even those who professed religion were filled with hatred for those who were the slightest bit different from themselves. "Joshua has given us all a new and beautiful vision of life and helped us to see that no one is a stranger," was the way Soad described Joshua's effect on people.

Shlomo was again invited to lead the singing. This man was so unassuming and self-effacing, and expressed such sincere love for everyone, no matter what their religion or race, that everyone loved him and looked forward to his performing at each gathering. The Arab children were particularly fond of him. He always singled them out and showed them special affection. In his spare time he was teaching Arab children to play the guitar and make up their own songs.

Aaron introduced Joshua this time, and to Joshua's embarrassment, revealed some remarkable things about him.

"The first time we all met Joshua, we were on a three-day furlough. Susan, Nathan, Samuel, myself, and some others bumped into him on the Mount of Olives. Not knowing much about the sites, we asked this stranger who seemed to be knowledgeable, and he kindly explained them to us. He seemed so ordinary. When we said good-bye, it never occurred to us we would ever see him again.

"Now that he has become one of us, each day we learn

more and more about him. His life is like a rose unfolding. This past week some tragic events occurred, and our friend was severely injured. What was remarkable was that he showed no trace of anger or hostility for those who perpetrated the vicious act. He showed us all in a very graphic way that he not only preaches to us, but lives what he preaches. Indeed, in getting to know him the way we have, he seems to be utterly incapable of taking offense at anything anyone does to him. I know what I have said embarrasses him, but I felt it proper to tell you. We have all had clergy preach pious things to us, only to be disillusioned to see that it was mere words they themselves never practiced. We have for our beautiful teacher a man whose words are his very life. To watch him each day is a living sermon. I tell you this so you can feel confident that you are not following someone who just says pleasant things, or a captain who merely sends his troops into battle, but one who leads them into the thick of the fight and is an inspiration to all.

"Joshua," Aaron said, turning toward him, "I know I have caused you to blush, forgive me. I wanted everyone to know how proud we are to have you as our teacher. Now, please come forward and speak to us."

"Aaron, you are without shame," Joshua said as he stood at the podium. "You make ordinary things seem so dramatic, you almost had me believing you. I am grateful to you, Aaron, and to all my friends who have helped me. You are truly good friends."

Then, turning toward the vast crowd spread out before him, Joshua began to speak. "My dear friends, I have heard recently of the many wonderful things you have been doing in your communities. You have been practicing all the things we have been speaking about, and you can already see the rich harvest you are reaping. Your goodness and love has spread like a fire in dry grass. Old relationships have been renewed, new friendships have been cultivated. People who were once unfriendly or hostile have responded to your genuine expressions of concern and interest in them and have now become your friends.

"Of late I have come across so many hurting people, and so much pain. I know you all endure hurt and pain and struggle with difficulty to understand it. I know life must be very confusing for you. But it is not senseless. There are patterns and reasons, though you may not be able to see them. It is important for you to know that your lives are not just an accident of circumstance or the products of random forces at work in the universe.

"Each of you is a masterpiece of God's creation. You were made special and are precious to God. He works each day quietly, calmly, within you, weaving together the apparently disconnected strands of your life. Your youth was a preparation for your life later on. As you grew older, each moment was part of the carefully planned training that God was putting you through, each day building on another, each of you being drawn along a path different from everyone else, because each of you is unique and special to God, with a special mission to accomplish for Him in this world, and a special message to preach through your life.

"There will always be pain in life and hurt. You cannot grow without it. Pain and suffering are the dark strands weaving through the tapestry of your life, providing the shadows that give depth and dimension to the masterpiece God is fashioning within you. Athletes embrace stress and pain as they prepare their bodies for the contest. You are made strong and refined through your hardships and struggles. They are not a punishment for sin. They are the necessary ingredients of life if you are to grow in God's image. If God is to mold the human clay of which you are made into something that resembles Himself, that process cannot help but be painful.

"So be patient! Know that your pain is not in vain, nor is it a punishment. God is too big to pick on people when, in

their weakness, they fall. When you do things that are hurtful, God, like a kind father, or more a tender mother, makes
adjustments in your life to remind you that your actions are
hurting others or yourself and prompts you to make
changes. But God is never cruel. He accepts you where
you are and is very patient as you turn ever so slowly back
to His love. He weaves everything, even your sins, into
good when you reach out to Him.

"Your life is really like a tapestry. You look at one side
and see all the disconnected and loose ends, and say, 'What
a mess my life is!' God sees the finished product on the
other side and sighs, 'How beautiful you have become!'

"So don't be discouraged or lose hope. Trust your Father
in heaven. He loves you more than you can imagine. Call
him Abba. He is truly your Daddy, so tender is His love for
you.

"He watches over your every deed, not to find fault or to
judge, but because He cares. This may seem impossible,
that He could be fully aware of every detail of your life, but
look upon the mind of God as the sun rising in the morning.
Its rays penetrate every detail of creation in a single
moment. God's mind is like that sunshine, touching and
penetrating all of creation in an instant. In this way He can
guide and enlighten you with His wisdom and inspire you
with His love.

"And do not be afraid to turn your children over to Him.
He is their Father and created them for a reason. He is
more concerned that they accomplish the purpose for which
He created them than you are and is determined they will
carry out His plan. So entrust your children to Him. He
will not disappoint you.

"May His peace and blessing go with you each day and
guide you in His own way, and along His own paths, and
may you always know that He is near."

When Joshua finished, there was no applause at first, just

silence as everyone was in deep thought. Then the vast crowd stood up and gave a thunderous ovation, much to Joshua's embarrassment.

Susan walked up to Joshua and hugged him, herself deeply moved by what she had just heard, tears rolling down her cheeks. Joshua kissed her tenderly on the cheek and stepped aside as she took the microphone.

When the crowd finally quieted down, she spoke.

"My dear friends, I really can't speak after that. Nothing more need be said. But a few words are in order. All of us who worked to prepare this day are most grateful to you for the sacrifices you all made to be here today, in spite of the boiling heat. Should you need anything, we would be more than happy to be of assistance. You can pick us out, as well as those who generously volunteered to help us, by the red armbands we are wearing. If we break now for our little picnic, we can continue in about an hour."

During the break, Joshua mingled with the crowd, talking to small groups and individuals. He seemed so ordinary and so casual, yet people were in absolute awe of him, as he looked at them and touched them so deeply that their lives would never be the same. As he spoke to them, each one had the same eerie feeling: "This man knows me. I just know it. When he looks at me I can tell he is looking down into the very depths of my soul and knows all about me. Yet he is not critical. He seems to be telling me, 'I know all about you, everything. I see your hurt and your struggle, and I understand. Do not be discouraged and do not give up. God loves you as you are, and I love you and want you to be my friend. I am your friend, and I will always be with you.'"

Each one felt the same way, and the realization changed their lives.

Then he would move on, briefly entering others' lives, bringing them healing and peace. Though all were touched profoundly, only they knew it. All the others were totally unaware of the profound change taking place throughout this vast crowd. A woman came up to him at one point excitedly holding up her large thermos container. Because of the heat of the day, her family had been drinking from the container since they arrived. Then she had noticed that they must have drunk three times the capacity of the container and it was still full. Joshua smiled and told her to keep it to herself. But then others noticed the same thing, and others, and still others, and before long pandemonium broke loose. But by that point, Joshua was nowhere to be found.

He had quietly slipped away until the snack time ended, then appeared with Aaron and the sheik and the others as the next session was about to begin. By then the crowd had calmed down.

The real climax of the day was the morning session. The afternoon was routine. Joshua spoke once more, briefly, then the crowd was dismissed. They had been instructed to contact their representative in the Knesset to work diligently for peace and in whatever way they could to pressure the prime minister and his cabinet to lay aside their hard-line platform and open their hearts to the misery and fear all around them, among their own people, and particularly in the ghettos, the refugee camps.

The crowd dispersed in a surprisingly quiet and orderly fashion. Joshua mingled among the people right to the end, leaving afterward with Sheik Ibrahim and Aaron and some of their families. Susan, Samuel, Nathan, and Daniel Sharon left with them and retired to the beautiful estate of Soad Avari's brother Elie for an evening meal and to rest.

That night was a most rewarding experience for everyone. Soad and Siavosh and Mathilde and Bill and Elie, and their friends Charli and Jamileh and Majid, shared plans they had for Joshua's dream of everyone working together. It was a generous undertaking brought about by a strange twist of fate. Both of these families were friends of Khalil, through their sons who had grown up together. After Khalil's conversion, all he would talk about was Joshua and the beautiful work he was trying to accomplish. Before long the two families became totally dedicated to Joshua's work and were avid Joshua disciples. Siavosh had already contacted his friends in Saudi Arabia and had traveled there to discuss with them his proposal. It was to develop a series of factories in various places with the intention of providing employment for both Arabs and Jews and whoever else needed work. The factories would contain research and development laboratories as well as training schools. The plants would have state-of-the-art equipment and would manufacture high-quality electronic products and then market them in the area and throughout the Middle East, gradually raising the living standards of all those affected. Their friends in Saudi Arabia at first laughed at the idea, thinking it was a joke, then when Siavosh pushed the proposal, they began to take it seriously and sat down to discuss it with him. He had to familiarize members of the royal family with the movement that Joshua and his friends had started and how widely it was spreading thoughout the country. As hard as it was for them to believe, they were finally convinced that as a business venture, and as long as it would help Arabs, it might be worthwhile to give it a try. They had lost fortunes on other less honorable ventures. This might just be something that could take hold and do some good for people for a change. It certainly would generate goodwill.

Charli and Jamileh had also contacted relatives in Lebanon to ask for their help. They insisted that Charli come and discuss the matter with them personally. He was to do that within the next week.

The sheik was impressed at the generous spirit of these people, and he offered his help. He was not as rich as the royal family, but his resources were considerable, and he wanted to make his modest contribution. Though he lived simply and still enjoyed the simple nomadic life, the sheik had a reputation as the wealthiest man in the country. At times, members of various royal families would go to him for short-term loans when secrecy was imperative.

The evening ended on a high note. No one could really believe all that had transpired ever since they had all become friends. Friends with high ideals working together can truly change the world. As the sheik and his family were leaving, the sheik took Joshua aside and quietly asked him if he had seen his son of late. Joshua could see the anguish in the man's heart.

"Yes, my friend," Joshua assured him. "As a matter of fact, he came to the meeting today with a large group of his friends and introduced them to me. Also, remember Soad Avari who spoke today? You know her family well. It was your son who interested her family and a considerable number of others in joining our group. He has done much for us. Be at peace, Sheik Ibrahim, your son is a changed man, and my Father is blessing his life because of your kindness in forgiving him and the great sacrifice you have made. Let your heart be at peace. You will soon be very proud of him."

"Thank you, my dear, dear friend," the sheik said, with grateful tears in his eyes. "I know you and Allah are very close, and that both of you watch over him. I am again indebted to you." With that the sheik walked down the path to the family's limousine that was waiting for him, and they drove off.

When the others left, Joshua stayed with the Avaris for the next few days and helped them formulate their grand undertaking.

16

IN THE DAYS that followed, the country was churning with activity. Much to the satisfaction of Aaron and the original organizers, the highly charged members of the Children of Peace, now deeply loyal to Joshua, were ready to carry out careful directions in laying a road for peace. A movement like this could easily get out of hand and become the tool of fanatical activists which would not effect its intended goal but merely polarize the society and add another layer of hostility.

But with Joshua's gentle leadership and the depth of his spirituality, his guidance spilled over into his followers, and they went forth armed with his peaceful spirit and deep sense of forgiveness for past wrongs. Government leaders began to feel the heat. Calm heads in the military also saw value to this new movement that seemed devoid of radical activists and operated with a coolheaded leadership. Only some of the Mossad felt distrust for the movement. They could not get a handle on it and contain it. They were still smarting over their debacle of a few weeks earlier and were angry over the protective guard Aaron and his friends had thrown around Joshua. Aaron had also, in the meantime, cleverly worked out an agreement with friends in higher places to restrain the Mossad and order them to leave Joshua in peace. They agreed, but Aaron's office would have to assume complete responsibility. With this he had no problem.

Newspapers were picking up the story and tracked down Aaron for an interview. Aaron contented himself with merely stating that a few friends of his had been trying to make some gesture to foster peace but had been getting nowhere. Joshua seemed literally to come out of thin air as an answer to their prayers. Almost single-handedly he forged together this whole movement by the beauty of his teachings and the sublimity of his messages, as well as the healing charisma of his personality. Soon Moslems and Jews and Christians were streaming to the gatherings from all over the country to listen to him. His message of healing and reconciliation appealed to everyone. "We are all sick of fighting and hatred," Aaron related to the reporters. "Only fanatics on both sides have the stomach to continue. And if we turn our country over to them, we will never have peace, because their sick minds feed on hostilities. It is a way of life with them. They are so filled with hatred and suspicion; conflict is their only relief."

"Where can we find this Joshua?" one of the reporters asked.

"He will be here tomorrow," Aaron told him. "You can come back and interview him then. I am sure he will be only too happy to meet with you."

The reporters left. Only one returned the next day, a Greek Jew by the name of Elias Seremetis. Joshua was there, and graciously acceded to his request for an interview.

"What is your full name, Joshua?" the reporter asked him.

"Joshua is all you need. That is what everyone calls me and that is what I go by," Joshua responded.

"Where do you live?" Elias asked him.

"I have lived in this land all my life, and wander from place to place," he answered simply.

"Don't you have a home?" the reporter continued.

"No, I have never needed one. Everyone is so kind to me," Joshua answered.

"Do you work? Do you have a job?" Elias asked.

"Yes, I bring a message of peace and good news to the people. Don't you think that's a full-time job?" Joshua answered, to the dismay of the reporter, who began to twist his long handlebar mustache.

"Yes, I can see that could be a full-time job if someone really took it seriously," Elias answered with a trace of embarrassment and cynicism. "Is it true the Mossad tried to stop your activities and even tried to kidnap you?" the reporter asked.

"You seem to have more information than I do. Why don't you tell me about it?" Joshua responded shrewdly.

"Isn't it true that Mossad agents kidnapped you?" Elias pursued.

"In truth, I can't say. The men didn't have any signs on them. They were strangers. Others may know who they were. But they didn't give me their names, so I really have no way of identifying them. Anyway the episode is over and we have since passed on from there. The significant thing is the profound desire the ordinary people have for peace. It is a shame leaders don't respond to the people's desires and establish a program of reconciliation which will bring all the people together the way God intended and create the climate where they can work and live side by side in peace. There is no room or justification for social or racial isolation in this complicated modern world. All God's children must realize they are the children of one Father and must work and live together in harmony. It was a beautiful testimony at our people's previous gathering to see Jews and Moslems and Christians meeting and praying together on the Temple Mount. To drive people out and then worship God by yourselves is a blasphemy against God and could not possibly make your worship pleasing to Him. These are lessons our people, Jews and Arabs, must learn to live by if there is to be peace."

"Don't you think this is just a bit naive?" Elias asked him.

"All dreams are simplistic and naive until you begin to put them into practice," Joshua answered. "Then you see how realistic they can become when there is goodwill to resolve the problems. Dreams are naive and simplistic only to the fainthearted and the cynics."

"Where do you intend to go with this movement, which obviously has considerable potential for either good or evil, depending upon your agenda?" the reporter asked.

"By its fruits you can tell," Joshua replied. "The people are being guided into a way that will lead to peace. It is inevitable. But prodding and pressure are necessary to instill courage where needed. In this we will not rest until all is accomplished."

The interview went well. The reporter, at first skeptical of Joshua's intentions and political skills, ended leaving deeply impressed, if not converted.

Later that week a frightful tragedy took place, which grieved Aaron and all his inner circle. Charli Mouawad had gone to Lebanon as planned. While he was there a vicious shelling occurred in the village he was visiting. A shell struck the house next door. People in neighboring houses escaped, but Charli went into the shelled house to rescue the trapped survivors, pulling six of them to safety before another shell struck, which killed him. His family was devastated when they received the news. Charli's mission, however, was not in vain. The people he saved were the family of those who were considering investing their money in Charli's venture. Out of gratitude they contacted his family and promised even more money than they had previously intended to give and said they would like to play a more active role in the project to help make it a reality as a memorial to Charli.

The episode was a sad note in the peace project that in all other aspects was flawless. The funeral for Charli took place in Lebanon. His family had a funeral Mass for him in Jerusalem, which Joshua, Aaron, Susan, and many of the others attended, an unusual sight, which would have been unheard-of only a few months before. Jewish friends even brought food for the family as well as mementos. The tragedy brought the group closer together than ever. Joshua assured the family that Charli's death was not in vain. He died as a martyr of charity, precious to God, and was now at peace with Him in paradise.

The next few weeks were on the surface uneventful, though ferment was growing everywhere. Then Elias's interview with Joshua hit like a bombshell. There were still millions who had not heard of the movement. The news story spread awareness of the movement everywhere, interesting many more people. Aaron's committee of key Jewish and Arab people was besieged with phone calls and inquiries, most excited in their enthusiasm about what they could do for peace. The inquiries came from both Arabs and Jews.

The effects of the news story, however, were not entirely positive. While the notoriety gave greater momentum to the movement, it also aroused the ire of the meaner elements in society, provoking them to plot countermeasures, furious at the thought that these "liberal activists" should dare attempt to bridge the chasm between Jews and Arabs. Hardly two weeks after Charli's death a strange thing happened.

A phone call came for Joshua at Aaron's house early one evening. The caller spoke in Arabic. Joshua answered in perfect Arabic, to Aaron and Esther's surprise. After the phone call, Joshua seemed sad.

"Joshua, what is the matter?" Esther asked, concerned.

"It is something I have to attend to. No need to be alarmed," he said to reassure her.

"Aaron, would you call Sheik Ibrahim?" Joshua asked. "I must talk with him."

Aaron called the sheik, then gave the phone to Joshua, who explained the phone call he had just received. The sheik agreed to meet him and promised to leave immediately.

"Aaron, would you drive me to the city? It is very important," Joshua asked.

"Of course, but what has happened? I am very concerned," Aaron asked.

"Aaron, there are some things I cannot share even with you who are so close to me. Life is not simple. Things that appear simple are not really simple, but are like threads in a finely woven tapestry with more ramifications than we could anticipate. God is aware of all of them and makes provisions for every contingency, even the most minute. Something tragic is about to happen, but you will get a rare glimpse into the beautiful ways of God. That is why I called Sheik Ibrahim."

"Joshua, you baffle me," Aaron complained. "Only months ago you were a stranger. Now you are a part of my life, and I still do not understand you any more than when you were a stranger. I can't fathom this mind of yours."

"Don't fret over it, my friend," Joshua told him. "You will put the pieces together one day, and it will make sense. I do appreciate your trust."

Before they left the house, Aaron contacted his staff officer and had him send an armed guard to follow them down the highway toward the city. Not feeling comfortable with this whole affair, he also left instructions for the guard to follow them to the site and reconnoiter the place when they arrived.

It was an out-of-the-way place where Joshua directed

Aaron, down near the dump in the Kidron Valley. As they arrived, the skeik was also arriving. Aaron ordered the guards to fan out and survey the area. Then, walking to the site the person on the phone had directed them to, they came to a ditch covered by a clump of low-growing shrubs. As they approached they could hear moans. Pushing aside the brush they found a figure lying in the ditch, badly beaten and bleeding profusely.

Aaron and Joshua went down into the ditch and gently lifted the body out of the hole onto soft ground. As soon as they placed him on the ground, the sheik cried out, "My son, my son! Khalil, my son!" The man fell to the ground and bent over the battered body of his son. Khalil's hands were tied behind him, and a note was pinned to his shirt. Pulling off the piece of paper, the sheik began to read it. It was clearly intended for Joshua.

"To the devil's son, and Satan's followers: Let this be a warning to all other traitors who turn against their brothers and collaborate with the despicable Jews, the enemies of our people. Death to traitors. Hell and eternal fire."

The note was signed "The soldiers of Allah."

Blood was pouring from Khalil's breast. He had been carefully stabbed to bleed to death slowly, with perfectly perverted timing so as to be alive to cause more pain to those who found him. The bizarre spirituality of fanatics "dedicated" to a loving God. That had to be the ultimate insult to God.

"Father, Father," Khalil said to his father as he reached out to touch him. The three men were kneeling by his side.

"What happened, my son?" his father asked.

"When I told all my friends about Joshua, many of them decided to follow him. They came to the last meeting and were touched by Joshua's words and his kindness. The others were angry and swore to punish me. They wanted me to tell them where they could ambush Joshua, but I wouldn't betray him. They beat me and I still would not tell them.   I was supposed to be bait, but when they saw the armed guards they fled just as you came."

"We must get him to the hospital immediately," Aaron said.

"No, I won't make it.   They made sure of that," Khalil said with weakening voice.

"Joshua, can't you do something to save my son?" the old man said imploringly.

Putting his arm around the sheik, Joshua told him, "Ibrahim, it is not my Father's will.   My Father has called your son home.   This very night he will be in paradise.   Your son has given his life for peace, and for God.   He is truly a martyr.   Let God take him home.   You will be with him soon and you will see the honor my Father will bestow upon your son."

"I love you, father," the dying man uttered faintly.   "I always tried to be true to you."

"I know, my son, you have been my special one, always loyal to me since you were a child.   Now it breaks my heart to see you broken like this."

"That's all right, father.   I know God is calling me.   I see His light, and I already know His peace.   He is beckoning to me."

"Good-bye, my son," the old man cried through his tears. "I will be with you soon."

"Thank you, Joshua, for giving me back to God and to my father," the boy said.

Joshua bent over him, saying quietly, as he kissed him on the forehead, "Go in peace to paradise, Khalil.   You will be welcomed with great joy."

Kahlil's hand fell from his father's grasp.   His father closed his eyes and kissed him.

Aaron called the guards down.   They took Khalil's body to their van and drove off to the hospital.

Joshua embraced the sheik and held the old man's trembling body.   He stepped back and looked into Joshua's eyes.

"Joshua," the sheik said, "I know all those boys who did this to my son. In the past, I would have had all of them killed. But now I feel no revenge, only pity for our troubled land and our people. And I know that is what my son would want. You have worked more miracles among us, Joshua, than you will ever know. And I do look forward to being with my son. Again you are right— I am deeply proud of him."

Joshua and Aaron both accompanied Sheik Ibrahim up the hill, assisting him as his feeble limbs faltered. Aaron invited the sheik to stay at his house. He declined. Joshua offered to go back home with the sheik. The old man thanked him but said he needed to be alone with his family. If Joshua would say a few words at the funeral, the family would be honored. Joshua nodded his willingness to do so.

The drive back to Aaron's house was long and sad.

"I can't help but feel for that old man," Aaron said. There was something touchingly beautiful about that cruel tragedy. How did you know what would happen there tonight, that you should call the sheik?"

"Some things you just know, my friend," Joshua answered.

"But you had to know that the boy would be there, and you also had to foresee the circumstances," Aaron continued. "Joshua, you are a mystery. I won't ask anymore, because I know you won't answer anyway. But what happened tonight was beautiful, as heartrending as it was. I feel honored to have been included."

"The sheik is a remarkable man," Joshua said. "He has seen much in his lifetime and has come a long way to understanding the mind of God. It was a difficult thing for him not to want revenge on his son's killers, especially knowing who they were. That is true godliness."

"I don't know whether I could have done the same. I was never taught to think that way," Aaron replied.

"Neither was the sheik," Joshua responded. "This represents a radical change for an old man who was just as militant as all the rest in his younger years. Maybe that is why he can forgive, because he understands them. It was a great comfort to know his son died such a hero's death. That healed a broken heart."

"Joshua, I hope there's no more tragedy," Aaron said. "It might scare people off, especially if they have families."

"It should be quiet for a while," Joshua said to reassure him. "There are many people in our family now, and you have to expect some incidents. It's a mark of success."

"Joshua, do you really think there is a heaven?" Aaron asked.

"Aaron, you could never imagine the beautiful things my Father has prepared for those who love Him," Joshua replied. "The beautiful things in this world are hints of the beauty of God's home. I do not think there is a heaven. I know there is a heaven, just as truly as you know there is a world all around you. God's creative power is not limited to the crass material things of earth. God has created things you would never dream of. One day you will see."

Not feeling comfortable on this territory, Aaron shifted gears. "How do you think our movement is going? Do you think we will attain our goals?" he asked.

"It seems we are moving in that direction," Joshua said. "The people have taken hold of the message and are carrying it in the right places. I have no doubt it will work."

Back home, Esther met them both at the door and could not wait to hear all the details of what had happened. Joshua said little. Aaron gave a detailed account of the whole episode, telling with tears how touched he was at the love between the sheik and his son, and what a beautiful ending to such a tragic life. Aaron found himself consoling

both himself and his wife by telling her the old man probably didn't have much time left and would be with his son
again soon. Esther looked at Joshua tenderly.

He just smiled.

CHAPTER **17**

T HE FUNERAL for Khalil was carried out with simple dignity. Although there were moments of traditional oriental wailing, there was an unusual note of joy that surrounded the ceremony. Sheik Ibrahim himself shed only a few tears and seemed strangely at peace during the whole affair, which set the tone for the rest of the family. People had come from all over the Middle East for the funeral. There were even representatives from royal families. The service was held at the Mosque of Omar. Aaron, Susan, Nathan, Daniel, and Samuel were present, as well as many other Jewish members of their organization who admired the sheik. Even the men who killed Khalil had the nerve to come. Whether it was from guilt or from curiosity or whatever other motive, they were there.

Joshua was asked to speak after the Imam delivered his sermon. Joshua's talk was very brief and delivered in beautiful, flowing Arabic.

"My dear people," he began, "few children have known such pain and anguish as this young man. His life was a tortured existence. Yet few will ever bring to their loved ones, and to the world around them, such a legacy of peace and hope for the future. This boy died at the hands of sick people, who will never know till they meet God the evil they have done." As Joshua said this he looked directly at the men who killed Khalil. They tried to stare him down but finally lowered their eyes in shame.

Then he continued, "The circumstances that led to his murder, and the moments surrounding his death, were so filled with heroism and godliness that his passing was precious even to God. The peace and joy that hovers over this assembly today is a striking testimony to the conversion that transformed Khalil's life into a herald of peace, which gives a new hope to all the people in our land. Few children have brought such hope to their parents in their last moments of agony. For parents to know that their son died in the arms of God is a rare blessing few can hope for. Khalil's parents have had that joy as well as the joy of knowing they will soon be reunited with their son. The beautiful way God brings good out of what appears to be evil and tragic! For those who believe, death is not a pitiful end. It is the beginning of a new and wonderful life.

"Everyone wonders what God is like. Khalil now sees Him. Everyone wonders what heaven is like. Khalil now walks through the streets of heaven, sharing with his new friends the joy and happiness of being in God's presence. This is a happy day for this young man. His pain is ended. He is now in a world of peace and endless joy. So while we mourn our loss, we rejoice in his happiness. That is the way it should be for those who have faith. Take heart and have faith. Your future is a little brighter because of this young man's sacrifice. Salaam."

After the ceremony, the sheik asked Joshua, Aaron, and their comrades if they would honor him by coming to his family's home where they intended to celebrate their son's going home to God. "This is a new practice for an old man, but I can truly say that I do rejoice in my son's death, or to be more positive, in his going home. I have you to thank for this, my young imam," the sheik said, as he patted Joshua's arm.

They all left together. The celebration that took place

that day was a precedent devoid of all remorse and vengeance or any trace of bitterness. The last moments of Khalil's life more than atoned for his troubled past and brought great honor to his whole family. It would be talked about for years to come.

In time word passed through the whole organization. Letters of condolence poured in to the sheik's family from all over the Holy Land, from Jews and Arabs and people of all beliefs. When everyone heard the story of this Arab boy's refusal to betray Joshua and his consequent martyrdom, it brought the group closer together than ever and even more determined to force a mind for peace on the stone-hearted leaders.

Then a strange, unexpected twist occurred, which made everyone pause.

The whole Arab community knew the identity of the men who killed Khalil. Joshua's Arab followers also knew and saw them frequently in public and never turned them in. The murderers were aware of this and were beginning to realize they had done a terrible deed and felt a profound shame, caused mostly by Joshua's community not betraying them. They also realized the sheik must know, yet he hadn't ordered their execution. Their confusion and guilt was a terrible punishment. To have to associate publicly with people who knew the mean thing they had done, yet were kind to them, was becoming almost unbearable. They even felt uncomfortable in their own homes, as many of their family members were followers of Joshua, and knew what they had done. Joshua's spirit of forgiveness was more devastating than a death sentence or a public flogging.

It was hardly a week after Khalil's funeral that the organization sponsored a rally for peace. It had been in the planning for weeks, unbeknownst to Aaron and his colleagues. The planners intentionally left them uninformed because of their positions in the government. Consequently, when they were called on the carpet, they could say in all honesty they knew nothing about the rally. It was an event that sprang spontaneously from the people's frustration with the way events were shaping up in the country.

Secretly, Israel's president was happy over the rally. He was trying, though without results, to encourage a more open and humane policy on the part of the government. The prime minister and his cabinet were furious. There had been rallies before, but this one represented such a cross section of society that one could say it truly represented the feelings of the vast majority of the populace, Jews and Arabs alike, something previously unheard-of in the country.

What was significant was the apolitical nature of the rally. All the banners and posters were simply marked, "We want peace, We want peace." No conditions, no other demands, just the statement of fact from the people themselves, a message that demanded to be heard, and accepted, and acted on.

A counterrally was organized a few days later by radical conservatives, but their fanaticism and bizarre appearance made them look more like a farce than a serious contribution to civilization. If government leaders identified with that group it showed dramatically how out of touch with reality they really were.

Events were accelerating now, and a host of undertakings were launched. Contacts with people in high places made it possible to get the buildings under way for the development projects that would provide jobs and needed products for consumers as well as income for the country. There were not many Arab-run operations like this in the land. Initial resistance was overcome because of the caliber and reputations of the persons sponsoring the projects. In a matter of months they were off the ground, and after a slow start, production mushroomed. Majid proved a master in organizing production lines and had his family's factory running like a top in no time at all. The Avari-Zanbaghe plant was much larger and under the shrewd management of a family friend, Ben Lautenschlager. Production was way ahead of schedule. Elie's contacts throughout the Middle East and other places brought in lucrative contracts for finished products from both operations. Employment increased, with Jews and Arabs working side by side and enjoying it. The sponsors were so happy with the results even from a business point of view that they began planning for other factories in the near future in other areas of the country.

These and other projects were quietly taking place while the organization was busy gaining new recruits and developing more awareness centers throughout the country, applying pressure on Arab as well as Jewish hard-liners. It was this balance sprung from genuine concern and care for people that made the movement so effective. Its strategy was being executed with almost military efficiency.

Joshua was spending his time behind the scenes but still active by keeping in touch with key friends in the movement, advising, focusing, counseling, prompting his followers to be careful not to take sides on issues but to show genuine concern for people everywhere so no one could accuse them of being divisive or political or partisan. "Peacemakers," he said, "must love everyone and not pit one segment of society against another or they will not be worthy to be called the blessed children of God."

Occasionally Joshua would take trips to Mount Carmel to visit Father Elias Friedman and talk to the many people who came out of curiosity to visit the sacred shrines there. Being a loyal Jew, the priest took care to instill in his Jewish visitors a deep reverence for their religious traditions. He was also thrilled to see Joshua visit their monastery and spend time with the monks.

Joshua also visited, with Aaron and Esther and the children, Rabbi Herbstman in Tel Aviv. Attending his synagogue, Joshua felt very much at home. Bernie's talks were about God and about those things that were of genuine concern to God. His relentless endeavor was to develop a deep spirituality in the hearts of his flock. Joshua also enjoyed his keen, quiet sense of humor that had the congregation rolling with laughter in the midst of the most serious talk on spirituality. "All holy people should have his humor," Joshua told Aaron and Esther as they were leaving the service one Friday evening.

One day as Aaron was taking Joshua and his family for a ride, they drove through the Plain of Esdraelon, the site of so many historic battles. Aaron made the flippant remark, "If your crowds get any larger, we may have to have our future meetings here in the ancient battlefield, with all its connotations for the Armageddon."

"You jest, Aaron," Joshua replied, "but the next crowd is going to be so large it might not be a bad idea to consider this place. We don't have many options left."

"Are you serious?" Aaron asked.

"I expect there might be somewhere close to thirty thousand people at the next gathering," Joshua answered. "People are getting desperate for peace and are beginning to feel this is their last chance. They are ready to cooperate with whoever will seriously work to end the conflict and the constant tension."

"Maybe this might be a good place to meet," Aaron said. "There is plenty of space. Susan will hate making preparations for a site this far away. But you are right, we may not have a choice."

As they drove along, Aaron suggested to Joshua that he organize his followers into a more permanent community. The movement was now widespread, and it was obvious the people were coming back not just because of their interest in peace but because they were starving for the kind of spiritual sustenance Joshua was giving them.

"You really have to organize them into something more permanent," Aaron told him frankly. "They will not leave you, Joshua. If we found peace tomorrow, these people would still come after you. We are truly your disciples now, and you are really God's presence for us. We need you; in fact, the whole world needs what you have to give."

Joshua listened thoughtfully, saying nothing for the longest time. Then, finally, he answered, "Aaron, I have taught you and Esther and Nathan and Samuel as well as Susan and Daniel and Rabbi Herbstman and Father Elias many things while we were together on private occasions. I also met with Elie and Soad and Mathilde and Sheik Ibrahim and taught them many things I did not teach the others. You have all been well prepared. Father Elias is well trained and well prepared to give guidance where there are questions. I leave it to all of you to pass on my message and to spread it to others. I will always be by your side and in your hearts. Do not be afraid of the future. Leave that to my Father. That is His problem. Let today take care of itself."

"What are you saying, that you're leaving?" Aaron replied. "Joshua, I can never figure you out. Can't you ever answer a question in a way I can understand? You're impossible."

"Oh, Aaron, stop worrying! Why can't you just enjoy today and be happy we are all together right now? Tomorrow will take care of itself."

It was not that Joshua had not anticipated the problem. The group was growing to such proportions that it was becoming impossible to meet the way they had been. Joshua realized this and was quietly grooming his closest friends to carry on his message long after the present problems ceased. But he saw no point in creating a problem within the group before their peace project was completed. That would still take time, as the truly powerful people on either side lacked the grandeur of soul or the wisdom of spirit to rise above the petty squabbles of infantile feuding in order to reach out and offer a compromise based on a workable partnership rather than an icy standoff at borders waiting for a pretext to pounce on one another. A partnership, Joshua knew, was the only compromise that made sense. The Arabs had the money. The Jews had the technology and the expertise. Why not work together in joint development and business ventures, like the two projects already started?

The peace movement was a plum for the opposition party, who had been pushing for peace in season and out of season. It was only blunders on the part of Arabs that had thrown them out of office years back. But now the climate was ripe again. This put extraordinary pressure on the present government to come up with something other than a mere gesture for peace. The prime minister held a special meeting of his cabinet. Hard-liners under pressure become more irrational and intransigent than ever, and this time they were no different. The prime minister, afraid of losing his job if he gave in to demands for peace, was in a state of paralysis. Unwilling to lose the support of the radical right, he could offer nothing of any real value to the people. In his heart he would like to be the champion of peace with dignity and strength but was not willing to sacrifice his political office to accomplish it. The meeting ended in anger with no decision.

Outside, the demonstrations were larger and more persistent with each passing day. What the prime minister did not realize was that if he had the courage to make a sensible decision in spite of the radicals, he would not have to worry about his job. He could count on the vast support of the people who would be behind him all the way. This way eventually his government would fall and new elections would sweep him back into power with a strong mandate for peace with dignity and solid defense. Everything was in place for a new government to form lucrative technical, industrial, and agricultural partnerships with Arab residents and Arab investors from neighboring countries. From there on the potential was mind-boggling. The natural markets for goods made in the Holy Land were Arab neighbors. With these markets undeveloped, the country could survive only with the help of goodwill offerings from friends.

The peace movement had forced a stalemate with the government. No one could predict what turn events would take. Aaron apprised Joshua of the situation and asked if he had any insights into what would happen next. Joshua's answer as usual was unsatisfying. "Be patient, everything unfolds in due season."

The demonstrations never let up. Day after day, incessant chants for peace were enough to unnerve the most calculating and calloused politician. Joshua did not even ask Aaron for information, nor did he read the newspapers. He met with the sheik, Aaron, and his friends on a daily basis, talking to them about the future, sharing with them his vision of God and the love the disciples should have for one another, and encouraging them to be towers of strength to the people as time went on. The sheik felt honored Joshua picked him in spite of his old age to be part of his inner circle. Each of those he picked had imbibed Joshua's spirit fully and were well prepared to carry on that spirit.

The time came for the next gathering. Everyone was fired up for this one. The Plain of Esdraelon was out of the way, but since people were coming from all over, and the country was small, it was no more than an hour's ride from even the farthest places.

On the way there, Joshua told the story to Aaron's children and the sheik's grandchildren of the great battle that took place during the reign of King Zedekiah in the time of Jeremiah the prophet. Hundreds of chariots and tens of thousands of soldiers lined up on either side of the battlefield and met head-on. Thousands lay dead and wounded in the field, a tragic waste of human life, and all because the people cut God out of their lives and chose to live independently of Him and worship gods of their own fashioning.

The children's vivid imaginations had no trouble filling in all the details. The vast plain that stretched before their eyes provided a dramatic panorama for replaying the whole battle scene from beginning to end. Joshua answered their endless questions, leading one of the children to ask him, "How do you know so much about the battle—were you there?"

Joshua answered whimsically, "Yes, right there watching the whole thing."

Susan and the others, including Soad and Jamileh and Elie, had arrived and were busy organizing the volunteers when Aaron and Joshua drove up. The acoustics people had come the day before and set up the complex sound system and tested it out. They stayed overnight in the organization's rented trailer to protect their equipment.

People had been encouraged to come in buses to ease the parking burden. They were arriving in a continual flow. Many were newcomers and were anxious to meet Joshua, who made himself readily accessible. Crowds flocked around him right up until the program started. His easy ways and unassuming manner put everyone at ease. People felt they had known him all their life and remarked at how comfortable he made everyone feel. It was almost like talking to a long-lost friend.

The format for the program was the same as the previous ones. There was nothing grandiose, nothing of the theatrical. People did not come to be entertained. They came for a purpose. They came for peace, peace within their own hearts and peace in the world in which they lived. Joshua, they knew, had the key to that peace, and they came to hear him and follow him.

Joshua's effect on people was so profound, it didn't take long before they began to wonder about him and who he was. Charismatic personalities affect others at a level that is almost mystical, causing people to attribute to them characteristics that transcend the merely human. Joshua's effect went beyond even that, especially after word circulated about the two children shot in the street, and the Arab girl hit by the speeding car, and the incident of the drinking water at the last gathering. People would approach Joshua just to touch his clothes, or to have him touch their children, or themselves. Many said they were healed after Joshua touched them, some from physical ailments, others from emotional problems. Whether this was true or imagined is not possible to ascertain, but what was true was that his followers' love of him knew no bounds, whether they were Jews, Moslems, Christians, or whatever.

Those closest to Joshua, however, had their own ideas about Joshua. Nathan, supposedly so cynical, had discussed the matter over lunch with Aaron and Daniel, with whom he worked. Nathan had been watching Joshua like a hawk and noticed little things about him that eluded the others, like Joshua's ability to understand things before they happened. He concluded this from noticing that Joshua was never really surprised at anything new or surprising that occurred. He also noticed Joshua calling people by name before he was introduced to them. Joshua's intimate identification with biblical sites fascinated him. He had also caught Joshua a few times at prayer, his whole being completely transformed. He had no doubt but that Joshua was truly communicating with his Father, and his Father was answering him. He himself felt he was on sacred ground just being there. It was an eerie feeling. Aaron, too, had incidents to contribute, really intimate ones culled from the hundreds of little things Joshua did during the long time spent at his home. Daniel also had his ideas. He never got over Joshua's warning him about the car bomb.

All in all the little circle, although they could not put together what they felt about Joshua, sensed there was something sacred about his presence and felt that God had, for some precious purpose, placed him in their lives. They all felt honored and privileged that he should be so specially close to them and their families.

By noontime, the gathering crowd was already approaching thirty thousand, and there were still more coming. Concerned about possible disorder, Aaron had asked Joshua over a week before if he should assign troops to be present just in case. Joshua just laughed and said not to worry. There would be no disorder.

The program began a little late. Shlomo was present again and only too happy to provide the music. This time, however, he had a partner, a blind Arab singer, a girl named Fatima. She had been blinded by soldiers' bullets when troops raided the refugee camp where her family lived. She had a rich soprano voice that rang with such pathos and sincerity that it touched the hearts of everyone. Sheik Ibrahim was there on the platform with the other members of Joshua's inner circle. Though appearing sad and pensive, he sat with great dignity. Soad and Jamileh and Elie sat near him. Off to the side of the platform was Elias Seremetis, with his camera, taking shots of all the important people present, and every now and then twisting his long waxed mustache.

Finally, Joshua was introduced. The applause was thunderous. When he rose to speak, he looked so unpretentious and unassuming. It was as if he were not even aware that this whole crowd would do his slightest beckoning.

"My dear people," he began, as was his custom, "we have grown from such humble beginnings. Those who dreamed this vision long ago, Aaron and Susan and Daniel and Nathan and Samuel, and those who responded so willingly, Sheik Ibrahim and his family and friends, all deserve our respect and our gratitude for what has taken place during the past several months. It is truly the work of God. You yourselves are no small part of what God is accomplishing in your midst. It is a beautiful work.

"We have watched from a distance what you have been doing and how you have conducted yourselves. Your behavior has been beyond reproach. I myself am proud of you.

"I know you all carry many burdens. Many have lost parents and children in the terrible slaughter of times past. Many of you are newcomers to our land and have left behind family and dear friends. I know your pain and your loneliness and the trials you face even here. Some of you are without a home and unemployed. Many of you nurse old and painful wounds. Others have been victims of cruel injustice right here in your own lands. I feel your hurt in my own heart and carry the pain of your anguish. I have watched you grow to rise above that pain and let it go. I have seen you reaching out to others who were hurting, trying to ease the burden of their pain. In doing this you forgot your own anguish, and opened your hearts to receive God's blessing and the comfort of His presence within you. You have grown immensely in the spirit of God.

"You have also freed yourselves from bitterness and hatred and in the beautiful spirit of God's forgiveness have befriended one another in a truly sublime expression of divine love. This has not been easy, nor will it be easy in the future. But do not lose heart. Even when your gestures of goodwill are not appreciated, do not take offense. Continue to do good. You are not doing good for praise or for appreciation. You are doing good because goodness is a part of you and you are expressing what is within you. Never weary of doing good and never tire of forgiving. Goodness will win out in time.

"In your demonstrations, you have been quiet and restrained. Continue that way. Words and loud noises are of little value. Your silence is deafening. Your peacefulness touches hearts and opens minds. Never resort to bizarre behavior or illegal acts. They tarnish the simplicity and the purity of your message and distract people from your true purpose. They create other issues and polarize those who would otherwise support you.

"Know that God is always by your side and in your hearts. Love one another, my dear friends, and know that I will always be with you. When you love one another, my Father and I will come and live within you and bring you peace. Keep high your ideals. Teach your children to love. Do not pass on to them your hurts and your grief. They cannot bear it without damaging their lives irreparably. Teach them to be free and not be afraid to trust.

"My faithful friends Aaron, Susan, Nathan, Samuel, Sheik Ibrahim, Soad, Jamileh, Father Elias, Rabbi Bernard, Elie, Mathilde, I have spent many hours with them, teaching them, guiding them. They are your teachers. Listen to them. They will not lead you astray.

"There are among us today four very special young men. They are very special to me. They do not know that I knew, but I did know, that they saved my life. They were assigned a very difficult mission by their grandfather, Sheik Ibrahim. They were assigned to watch me so nothing would happen to me. They did their job well. I was not supposed to know about it, but I did. I was aware of their presence every moment, and I am deeply grateful to these four heroic young men. Daoud, Najah, Ali, and Mahmoud, please step up here and let me thank you.

The boys looked up at their grandfather as if to ask for permission to go forward. He was beaming from ear to ear and shook his head, signaling them to step up. When they reached the platform, the crowd drew their breath in awe at seeing four little boys, hardly fifteen years old, who had such a frightening assignment. Joshua hugged each of them and gave them a present, a figurine he had carved, a perfect replica of himself, as a symbol that he would never forget them and did not want them ever to forget him. The boys blushed, and as the sheik stood up, they walked over to him and he kissed each of them. The people clapped for almost three minutes while the boys went back to their places.

Joshua continued with his talk. "My message to you today is: stay the course. Continue on your way and do not lose heart. You are doing the work of God, and He will not allow you to fail. That is certain. Your work is likened to a wise man who was growing old. His time was running out and he was concerned about his children. Times were bad and the old man had little left to provide for them. The old man's neighbors were miserable people and he could not trust them to be kind to his children when he died, even though their children were his children's playmates.

"The wise old man called in his own children as well as his neighbors' children and sat them down. Taking a sack out of the closet, he confided to them a secret. In the hills not far from their home was a very large field which he owned. The old man opened the sack and took out a handful of nuts that looked like acorns. 'You see these nuts?' the old man asked. 'Well, listen to me. I have nothing to give you but these. And you, my neighbors' children, are like my own. Each day I will give each of you a bag of these nuts. You are to go up into the hills and plant them. The next day I will give you more. And each day after that until the sacks are empty. And you are to keep this secret to yourselves.'

"Years later, the wise old man died. The neighbors were mean to the old man's children and tried to turn their children against them. In time the neighbors died, and the children were left alone. Being poor and having nowhere to earn a living, the children said to one another, 'Remember the wise old man, our father, how he gave us the bags of nuts to plant? Let us go to see what has happened to them.' They went up to the hills overlooking the valley, and to their surprise, there before their eyes was a vast forest of tall, beautiful, and rare trees, stretching as far as the eye could see, a rich treasure that would make them all extremely wealthy. However, in order to gather that wealth they had to be forever friends and work together on a piece of land that before was useless.

"And that, my friends, is the way it is here in our land, like the treasure the wise old man gave to all his children— to reap the treasures you must work together. May the wise old Father's peace and blessing be always in your hearts and may you always love one another. Salaam, shalom."

The vast crowd was stunned at the tone of finality in Joshua's message and stood for a moment in silence, then let out a thunderous ovation which lasted for over five minutes. Aaron had a difficult time quieting the crowd. In fact he had a difficult time calming himself. Strong man that he was, the tears kept rolling down his cheeks each time he approached the microphone to speak. No one else on the platform could help him as they were all crying as well. Whatever it was that Joshua said, it touched them all profoundly, and they could not restrain the force of their feelings. The whole vast crowd was just as deeply shaken, and spontaneously began to shout out, "Blessed is he who comes in the name of the Lord, Hosanna, Hosanna, Hosanna to the son of David." Never had they heard anyone speak the way this man spoke, and it touched the very core of their being.

During the break, Joshua mingled with the crowd. They clung to him as if he were to disappear. When he looked into each one's eyes, his look spoke volumes and healed many wounds and changed many lives. They could see in those eyes the love of God. In spite of their past lives for which they had long repented, and what they thought of themselves, they knew God loved them. That realization alone brought powerful healing.

As Joshua walked through the crowd, many asked if they would see him again. He told them not to worry, they would see him again, and that it was important for them to nourish the good relationships they had struck with all their new friends, and that they should help one another, particularly during difficult times. God was pleased when people lived like a family and not in isolated existences, because people needed one another.

The remainder of the session was routine. Instructions were given to the group before they left, and they were encouraged to be persistent in their efforts for peace, not become frustrated or tempted to resort to desperate means. Their most powerful asset was their unity and calm persistence and their unblemished behavior. They must let no one draw them off guard into illegal or violent acts. Help one another, care for one another. That was the bond that cemented the whole group together into a family. No one was a stranger.

18

T HE RAPID GROWTH of the movement around Joshua was so dramatic it could not but cause concern among settlers in the occupied areas. They soon began to organize counterdemonstrations and attempted to draw Joshua's disciples into a confrontation, but to no avail. Aaron, Susan, and the sheik had appointed leaders whom they could trust for their prudence and patience and assigned them to lead the various groups around the country. They were a great influence in keeping the crowds calm at times when hostile instigators tried to start a brawl or bait Joshua's followers into doing something violent or illegal, in an attempt to discredit the movement. But the people's discipline was unshakable.

The meeting on the Plain of Esdraelon was the last of the big assemblies. The crowds were just too large. The members in various parts of the country now met in their own smaller groups, with their group leaders to guide them. Joshua had trained the leaders well in the quiet, private sessions he had with them. He was so casual about it, they did not even realize they were being trained for anything. However, by the time he had finished with them, they had so thoroughly absorbed his spirit, they were well prepared to go out and mold the people into a Joshua-like way of thinking and a Joshua-like way of acting. The people's own fond memories of the words of Joshua still moved their hearts and kept the fire alive and the memory of him fresh.

Aaron saw Joshua less and less. Nathan and Susan and the others were constantly calling Aaron to ask where he was, but he could give them no answer. Even the sheik did not see him, except on rare occasions. More and more word was coming back to Aaron and the others that Joshua had shown up in Tel Aviv or on the West Bank or in Haifa.

One such incident occurred while Father Elias was meeting with his group in Haifa. He had a large contingent of Joshua people in the area. They were not only a loyal group consisting of Arabs, Jews, and Christians, they were also a very influential group, who had powerful contacts within the Knesset and even in the cabinet. As they were meeting on this particular occasion, there was a knock at the door. When one of the people answered, they were shocked to see Joshua standing there. Of course they were thrilled that he came but were surprised that he even knew of the meeting. They immediately ushered him inside and properly seated him in a place of honor before continuing the meeting, then afterward invited him to speak.

"I have not come to give you a speech," he said, "but merely to encourage you in the new life you are living. The peace venture is only a temporary issue. The important thing is that you do not lose sight of the fact that you are now a new people, a new family. I am happy you have Father Elias to guide you. Trust him and accept his guidance. He will teach you all you have to know to find your way to God and to preserve your unity as a family. And remember I will be with you always, so do not lose heart."

After speaking briefly, while people were busy talking to one another, Joshua just seemed to have walked through their midst and slipped out of sight.

On another occasion, Rabbi Herbstman was telling Aaron how Joshua had shown up at a meeting he was having in Tel Aviv. He was at first stunned, though on thinking it over, realized he should not have been shocked because that was

just the way Joshua did things, unannounced and sponta-
neously. Aaron, curious as to the time and the date, asked
Bernie when it was Joshua had made his appearance.
When Bernie told him the exact time, Aaron was silent.
"What's the matter, Aaron?" Bernie asked him.

"What you have just told me is strange, because I got a
phone call from Samuel who was holding a meeting in Ein
Kerem at the same time and the same day, and he said
Joshua stopped in to visit with his group. I don't know what
to make of it."

"Are you sure it was the exact same time?" Bernie asked.

"Yes, I am certain," Aaron replied, baffled as to what was
happening. "Next time I see Joshua, I'm going to pin him
down and ask him point-blank. I feel we are friends enough
for me to be blunt with him and for him to be honest with
me. This is the most uncanny thing I have heard of in my
whole life, and me a physicist. Imagine trying to tell someone about this. They would think I'm an idiot who has lost
his screws."

"There is something very special about that man, Aaron,"
the rabbi said. "I don't know what it is, but I have the
strangest feeling when I am in his presence. I don't know
how to say it, but I feel there is something sacred about
him. Yet he is so human and so natural, and so much fun to
be with."

"I know, and to think that he sleeps in our house," Aaron
responded. "I've wondered more than once."

The other groups around the country had similar brief
visits from Joshua. He was always pleasant and friendly. If
they doubted their senses when they saw him, touching him
convinced them he was real. His message was always similar, though varying at times according to the needs of the
group.

Finally Joshua showed up at Aaron's door. He must have
known he was in for a thorough grilling, because as soon as
Aaron answered the door, Joshua greeted him with a broad

grin and commented on how busy Aaron had been of late.

"You're darned right I've been busy, trying to track you down," Aaron shot back, half in humor and half in bewilderment. "I hear you've got a new trick lately, being in two places at the same time. Joshua, you push our friendship to the ultimate limits. I can't keep up with you."

"Aaron, don't be so upset. You know with all that has to be done, I can't check in with you over every move I make. You have to know I'm trying to accomplish the impossible already, and it can't be done in just ordinary ways. Relax and just enjoy the fun. Well, are you going to make me stand out here all night or do you think you might invite me in?"

"Oh, I'm sorry, Joshua. You distracted me. Come right in. We were just sitting down for supper. Esther said she thought you might stop by, so she made some extra. Apparently a woman's intuition can get a better handle on you than my military training."

"Joshua's here!" the children cried out in unison, as they ran out to greet him. "We missed you, Joshua. We're so glad you're back."

"Yes, Joshua's here," their father answered. "At least the children are glad to see you."

Joshua realized this was all Aaron's ironic sense of humor. He was actually happier to see Joshua than anyone. He was just feeling sad that Joshua's time with them seemed to be coming to an end, and the thought of it hurt.

As the family was well into the meal, Aaron told Joshua some good news. "I've been waiting for weeks to tell you this, but I couldn't find you. Elie's brother-in-law, Siavosh Avari, came to talk to me. His family is very pleased with the progress of the factories and not only are they planning to build others, but they have a remarkable idea. Siavosh and Elie came over to test it on me. Their family is very close to King Fahd. Inspired by Joshua's idea of working together, they thought maybe they would make an appointment for an audience with the king and lay a proposal before him. Saudi Arabia and the other Arab countries, with all their oil money, are having a difficult time developing their countries. Our country on the other hand is always broke but has the genius and technology everyone needs. It is a natural complement. They need one another. With the success the Zanbaghe-Avari factories have been having, Siavosh and Elie thought they would try to interest the king in a joint venture with our country. It would be the salvation of the Arab people within our borders and would force everyone to work together and act as neighbors for a change."

"I think that is a wonderful idea," Joshua said, excited about the proposal. "When are they meeting with the king?"

"Sometime this week, I think," Aaron replied. "They had no trouble arranging for the audience. Sheik Ibrahim is a personal friend of King Fahd, and he is going with them."

"Well, that is something we will all have to pray over, because there will have to be considerable face-saving all around," Joshua responded. "It certainly does make a lot of sense."

The weeks that followed saw a continual buildup of support for the peace movement. The pressure on the prime minister increased accordingly, so did demands for further settlements on the West Bank. It was only the restraining power of Joshua's teachings that prevented the situation from exploding into open violence.

Siavosh, Elie, and the sheik returned from their visit with the king and were enthusiastic as they relayed the whole story to Aaron, Susan, and the others. The king had listened and sat very thoughtfully through the entire proposal. His brow furrowed several times as he thought of what it would take for him personally to enter into such an enterprise. At the end he said he would like to talk it over with some of his close allies whose counsel he could trust and whose support would be critical. The sheik's presence made it difficult for the king to say no outright and prompted him to consider the whole proposal in depth, since the sheik thought it worthwhile.

The king did have a difficult problem with the undertaking. He could not see himself dealing directly with these people who were treating his Arab brothers and sisters so harshly. He reminded his guests that the Jews in Spain had prospered under the Moors, and "now look how they treat our people. It is very difficult for me to even consider helping them."

"But Your Majesty," Sheik Ibrahim assured him, "you will be nicely forcing them to undertake a venture that will make it possible for our people to live in dignity and to play a major role in the future of the country. That has all kinds of potential. And you will be looked upon as the savior of our people. Not only will you be helping our own people immediately, you will be the catalyst for bringing prosperity to Arabs throughout the whole Middle East."

The king began to see some merit to the idea and admitted the proposal had some interesting long-term ramifications. He promised to consider the matter without delay and let them know his answer within the week. After their audience, the king invited his old friends to have lunch with him. Later in the afternoon they returned home.

The group's reaction was one of delight. The possibilities were mind-boggling. Joshua himself was optimistic. But they still had to wait for the king's reply.

To their surprise they did not have to wait long. Hardly a week after their audience with the king they received a request from King Fahd to come back and meet with him again. They wasted no time and were there by the next day.

The king had talked with his advisers and with other Arab leaders. They liked the idea, because it was a positive way of helping Arab people directly, but they thought it would be out of place for the king to be directly involved.

After much thought and a couple of sleepless nights, the king came up with a solution. They would use their well-respected contacts in Holland to act as intermediaries. This would save face for everyone and make it possible to get the projects off the ground.

The remaining problem was this: Who would make the initial contacts with Jewish officials? The sheik offered to approach the prime minister and inform him of the king's interest in meeting with him. The king thought that a good idea and suggested that for follow-up one of his personal representatives could then meet with the prime minister or his representative. With that much decided upon, the three men returned home to share their good news.

The sheik met with the prime minister, and after a long and tedious session, the prime minister agreed to receive a representative from King Fahd. The meeting took place a short time later, and after a full two days of secret talks with top advisers, the prime minister decided to go ahead with the project. He knew the proposal would infuriate his radical right supporters, but this time he could afford to ignore them, because this proposal was so far-reaching and would be of such massive benefit to the whole country he could survive without their support. He knew the whole population would ultimately support him on this one.

The king was humble enough to agree to the trip to meet with the prime minister and sign the agreements. The day of the signing was kept a secret, so there was no time for any opposition groups to mar the day with raucous protests or worse. The evening television carried the story, and within hours the whole country was in a frenzy. Most people could not believe it. Joshua's people were ecstatic. The sheik was an immediate national hero. Aaron and Susan and their colleagues were no longer suspect but were invited to dinner at the prime minister's home. The radical right were beside themselves with rage. For them it was treason and spelled total rejection of everything they held

sacred. Just the thought of having to exist side by side forever with Arabs and to see them as equal partners in society, in business, in every aspect of life was a humiliation so
monumental they could not even conceive of it as being
possible. To these fanatics, the insidious betrayal by the
government was tantamount to giving official recognition to
the Canaanites of old, whom, to their way of thinking, God
had ordered to be eliminated.

Needless to say, they brought about the fall of the government. The prime minister anticipated this, and new
elections were scheduled. The prime minister won by a
comfortable majority, which put the radical right forever out
of the picture. Joshua was unsurprised. He knew that no
society can long survive with people like that. They have
no worthwhile contributions to make to civilization. They
put society in deep freeze and muzzle creativity and innova-
tion and obstruct decent people from solving the dreadful
problems facing our civilization.

Negotiations now had to be conducted with the money
people. The Dutch intermediaries were seen almost daily
meeting government officials and bankers as details of the
complex financing arrangements were being made. Siavosh
and Elie and the Mouawads attended all the meetings as
they would be the prime agents for setting up this whole
operation throughout the country.

The agriculture minister was in heaven at the newfound
international position he held. It was his assignment to
work with the Saudis in sharing the imaginative techniques
for making the desert flourish. A multitude of new jobs was
created which gave hope to highly trained engineers and
doctors and technicians pouring into the country from
Russia, who previously were wandering the streets all but
homeless and hopeless.

The whole country, in fact, had a new life and a new
hope. People could not believe that such a cataclysmic
undertaking could happen almost unnoticed and overnight.

The radicals on both sides were unhappy. They would always be there. Sometimes Joshua got the feeling they were born that way and were that way as children. Political or theological principles had nothing to do with their behavior. Their problem was purely psychological and should they one day find their way to heaven, their response would probably be pretty much the same, negative and critical: "Oh, is this all there is, God? What a disappointment!" Then, Joshua thought, they would begin to spell out in detail all the things God could have done in designing heaven.

CHAPTER 19

DURING ALL this flurry of activity, Joshua was nowhere to be found. Aaron called all over the land. No one had seen him, not the sheik, nor Father Elias, nor Samuel, nor Susan, nor Rabbi Herbstman. No one. If anyone should have gotten the credit for this completely peaceful overthrow of a society, it was Joshua, and he had vanished. Aaron was furious. Even Esther, who was ordinarily imperturbable, was upset. She wanted more than anything to see him bask in the glory that was rightly his. Apparently that was unimportant to him. Even the Mossad had a change of heart and had half their home-based force scouring the country looking for him. He was nowhere.

Then one day a band of nomads coming in from the Negev stopped off to pay their respects to Sheik Ibrahim and told him of this strange group of Jewish and Arab children trekking through the desert, retracing Moses' steps. They were with a young man they called Joshua. He was dressed in ordinary shirt and khaki pants and was wearing desert headgear. A gold medallion hung around his neck, and he was carrying a canteen and a backpack. He looked like a Jew.

The sheik quickly asked in what direction they were heading. The travelers could not tell him for sure. It seemed they had just come from the hills and were traveling northeast.

Sheik Ibrahim immediately had a courier deliver the information to Aaron. There was little Aaron could do but wait until Joshua returned and then hope he would contact someone. On second thought he decided to send someone to catch up with him and stay with the group until they reached the city or wherever they were heading. At least they would have him within their grasp and would know his whereabouts. This way they could pick him up and meet with him on his return.

Two days later, Joshua showed up, invigorated and relaxed after his trip through the desert. They all met on Ben-Yehuda Street. He seemed totally unconcerned about what was taking place throughout the country, to the exasperation of everyone.

"Joshua," Samuel said, with a tone of disbelief, "don't you realize all the things that have been taking place around here the past few weeks?"

"What things?" Joshua asked calmly.

"Why, the whole country is in turmoil and all because of you, and you take off for the desert with a bunch of kids," Aaron said, beside himself in his inability to understand this man.

"Joshua," Esther told him quietly, "King Fahd accepted Siavosh and Elie and the sheik's proposal. The prime minister also accepted it. The government has fallen. New elections have been held, and the whole country has come to life with all the new construction projects. Our agriculture experts have gone to work in Saudi Arabia to set up farms throughout the desert."

"I think that is marvelous," Joshua said simply. "But what does that have to do with me?"

Exasperated at such total detachment, Nathan asked impatiently, "Well, isn't this what you were aiming at all along?"

"My sole aim was to encourage people to reach out to one another and treat each other as friends and open their hearts to God so He could guide them in the way of peace," Joshua answered.

"Well, this is how the people responded to your messages," Aaron said. "They took you seriously and accomplished a miracle. Aren't you excited about that?"

"Of course I am, Aaron," Joshua replied, "and I am also glad that my work is coming to a close. My part is done. The rest is up to yourselves entirely. And you will do a good job."

"What do you mean, coming to a close?" Susan said, with an air of annoyance and sadness. "You can't just drop out of sight after leading these people to the brink of revolution. Where do you intend to go?"

"Susan, my work is done. The revolution you speak of flows from the change in people's souls. It will not disrupt society. It will bring only peace. The people know what to do and where to go from here."

"You mean you are just leaving us?" she persisted, with tears in her eyes.

"I must go back to my Father," Joshua answered. "But don't be concerned. I will be with you always. You are very special to me. You are all my dear friends. I will always be by your side. Trust me. You will see me again. And we will all be happy together."

"Where are you going?" Esther asked.

At this point Nathan was growing impatient and interrupted the conversation with the remark, "Are you people so thick you don't realize yet what has been taking place in our midst? Joshua isn't just someone who happened to come in off the desert. I've been watching him for months now and I think I pretty well have him figured out. Read the old Gospels and see what you come up with. Then you won't need to ask any more questions. You will have the answers. Right, Joshua?"

"My Father loves you all in a very special way," Joshua told the group. "He saw your frustrating attempts to make a difference here and knew how difficult it was. He made His presence known to you in a powerful way to show you the path and bless your efforts. That has been accomplished now, and I must go."

"What about the children?" Esther asked. "You can't just leave them. They have grown so fond of you and are so attached to you."

"I will see them and talk to them. They will understand better than yourselves," he said. "I would also like to meet with our little group once more. They have all been so loyal."

Aaron agreed to make the arrangements.

After the meeting broke up, Joshua went home with Aaron and the next morning spoke to the children, telling them that he had been sent to do a job and now he had to leave.

"You are going back to God, aren't you, Joshua?" Mirza said bluntly.

"Yes, little one, my work is done," Joshua replied. "But I have something special for each of you." Wrapped in tissue were three wood-carved figurines just like the ones he gave the four Arab boys. "I want you to keep these as a reminder that I will always love you and watch over you."

The children were thrilled to receive the beautiful figures, and they took turns hugging and kissing Joshua.

After breakfast, Joshua blessed the family and, promising never to be far from them, left and walked down the street. Watching him till he disappeared, the whole family hugged one another, sobbing, and walked back into the house.

The meeting Aaron arranged for the others in the group took place only a few days later, where it all began, on the Mount of Olives. Aaron hosted their last supper at the Seven Arches. It was a repetition of the scene in Aaron's house. They were all brokenhearted to learn that this was the last they would see of their friend. But they realized his work was done, and they had to carry on the beautiful legacy he had given to them. The parting was tearful, but they were comforted by his promise never to be far from them. They could not understand how, but having such confidence in his words based on past experience, they trusted that if he made a promise he would keep it.

As they talked, church bells rang in the distance, a voice called out over loudspeakers beckoning Moslems to prayer, and a lone shofar announced the Sabbath. The coincidence reduced the group to silence. The setting sun cast its golden rays across Jerusalem. All eyes turned toward Joshua, who stood silently with a vision of the future, a tear in his eye, and a smile on his face. The impossible dream had come true.

Honest expression of goodness can dissolve hatreds, dissipate suspicions, allay fears, and transform ancient enmities into warm friendships. When that happens, no one can predict the forces that are unleashed upon society. When people saw the good generated by the factories and other projects spun off by the Joshua people, everyone was caught up in the enthusiasm. The phenomenon was indeed so simple that people could not help but wonder why someone did not think of the idea sooner. Though the idea may be simple, leading people out of a dark jungle of entangled, hate-filled emotions is a task that is beyond human capability. But once accomplished, the consequent events appear simple indeed.

The days that followed were filled with frenzied activity, as more factories were planned, conducted, and put on line. New housing was also needed. No more ghettos as in the past, but housing where people of wide differences were to live in the same neighborhoods. Only a handful objected. Those benefiting from the new housing were highly enthusiastic.

While some neighboring countries were slow to approve of the developments, decent people everywhere could not help but admire the vast changes that had taken place. The country was no longer a pariah, but truly the spearhead of a movement of cooperation that had the potential in time for bringing about the economic and cultural resurgence of the whole area.

Joshua's friends still met on a regular basis, no longer in peace demonstrations, but in much smaller groups with their leaders, who would discuss with them the many messages Joshua had given them. They kept alive Joshua's vision and told stories about this simple, wandering teacher, who by his love of God and belief in human goodness had changed forever the lives of the people who met him and listened to him. His goodness would live on in the hearts of those who followed him and would be passed on to the children, who were fascinated by the stories their parents told about him.

Not long after all these happenings, Sheik Ibrahim died. His funeral was carried out in elegant style. He wanted only a simple service, but the massive outpouring of affection from all the people necessitated a service that allowed for everyone, Jews, Arabs, and Christians, to weep and mourn their loss in a way that did honor not only to the sheik and his family for all that they had done but also to themselves for having risen above pettiness and vicious racial strife to bring about the transformation of their whole society. Before he died, the sheik requested of Aaron that his nephew, Jakoub, who lived on the farm in the Kidron Valley, might be appointed to his place in the Joshua community. Aaron was happy to accommodate him.

The story of Joshua and his brief sojourn among a tragic people may seem like a dream or a fantasy, and to some unreal or simplistic, but a dream is often nothing more than reality shorn of cynicism. Dreams have in the past come true where goodwill and determination overcame the obstacles and cleared the way for a new reality.